Praise for Jackson Pearce

Ellie, ENGINEER

"A charming book featuring an engineer who makes mistakes when navigating the roads of friendship." —*School Library Journal*

"Explicitly rejects the idea that activities and objects are gendered (e.g., boys and girls can both like engineering and tea parties). . . . A spirited, duplicable depiction of STEM fun." —*Kirkus Reviews*

"Pearce emphasizes Ellie's persistence and individuality. . . . Ellie's less-than-successful creations make for some funny moments." —*Publishers Weekly*

"The engaging storyline allows the reader to visualize how Ellie thinks in terms of STEM concepts while she's inventing, making this a perfect read aloud for STEM enthusiasts." —*School Library Connection*

"Ellie's easily relatable as an everyday kid. . . . Aspiring inventors will appreciate the descriptions and black and white sketches of Ellie's various creations." —*BCCB*

THE **DOUBLECROSS**

"Fast-paced, funny, and full of unexpected plot twists, this spy novel will easily appeal to middle grade adventure fans." —*School Library Journal*

"A zany, fun adventure, with Hale a kind and clever protagonist. Oddball characters with plenty of heart and nifty gadgets will draw in readers who appreciate humorous underdog stories." —*Booklist*

"Exciting missions, cool gadgets, and plenty of intrigue make this a fun read from the get-go. . . . International espionage plus wacky high jinks equals plot-twisting fun." —*Kirkus Reviews*

"An entertaining and memorable story." —*Publishers Weekly*

THE **INSIDE JOB**

"A fun-filled adventure from start to finish." —*Booklist*

"A funny, smart spy adventure with strong characters and clever twists." —*School Library Journal*

"This sequel will continue to thrill fans of the series. Wacky and action-packed." —*Kirkus Reviews*

Ellie, ENGINEER

Books by Jackson Pearce

JACKSON PEARCE

ILLUSTRATED BY
TUESDAY MOURNING

BLOOMSBURY
CHILDREN'S BOOKS
NEW YORK LONDON OXFORD NEW DELHI SYDNEY

BLOOMSBURY CHILDREN'S BOOKS
Bloomsbury Publishing Inc., part of Bloomsbury Publishing Plc
1385 Broadway, New York, NY 10018

BLOOMSBURY, BLOOMSBURY CHILDREN'S BOOKS, and the Diana logo are trademarks of
Bloomsbury Publishing Plc

First published in the United States of America in January 2018
by Bloomsbury Children's Books
Paperback edition published in November 2018

Bloomsbury books may be purchased for business or promotional use. For information on bulk
purchases please contact Macmillan Corporate and Premium Sales Department at
specialmarkets@macmillan.com

ISBN 978-1-68119-948-1 (paperback)

The Library of Congress has cataloged the hardcover edition as follows:
Names: Pearce, Jackson, author.
Title: Ellie, engineer / by Jackson Pearce.
Description: New York : Bloomsbury, 2018.
Summary: When Ellie, who loves to invent and build things, decides to build a doghouse as
a gift, she needs to get past the boys-against-girls neighborhood feud and ask for help.
Identifiers: LCCN 2017021570 (print) • LCCN 2017037525 (e-book)
ISBN 978-1-68119-519-3 (hardcover) • ISBN 978-1-68119-520-9 (e-book)
Subjects: | CYAC: Engineering—Fiction. | Building—Fiction. | Sex role—Fiction. |
Cooperativeness—Fiction.
Classification: LCC PZ7.P31482 Ell 2018 (print) | LCC PZ7.P31482 (e-book) | DCC [Fic]—dc23
LC record available at https://lccn.loc.gov/2017021570

Book design by Jeanette Levy
Typeset by Westchester Publishing Services
Printed and bound in the U.S.A. by Berryville Graphics Inc., Berryville, Virginia
2 4 6 8 10 9 7 5 3 1

All papers used by Bloomsbury Publishing Plc are natural, recyclable products
made from wood grown in well-managed forests. The manufacturing processes
conform to the environmental regulations of the country of origin.

To find out more about our authors and books visit www.bloomsbury.com
and sign up for our newsletters.

For my dad
(he's the best)

Chapter One

Ellie Bell was in her workshop.

Technically, it was a *playhouse*, because it was the little covered bit on her playset. But this was where Ellie *worked*, so that made it a workshop, if you asked her. And today, Ellie had a *lot* of work to do.

Ellie rattled her fingers inside one of the peanut butter jars full of screws and nuts and

bolts until she found what she was searching for—two slightly rusty bolts about the size of her dad's thumbnail. She looked out the window of the workshop. From this high, she could see over the fence and a few backyards over, to where the neighborhood boys were playing soccer. There was Dylan, who had giant feet, and the McClellan twins, who weren't allowed to eat any junk food (like *none*), and Toby Michaels. Toby Michaels was the worst. He was the bossiest kid Ellie knew, and she was in Mrs. Funderburk's third-grade class, so that was really saying something. That morning, when Ellie wanted to play soccer with them, the boys told her, "No, this is a boys' team."

(Which was really dumb since it wasn't a team at all, just a bunch of people in the neighborhood playing soccer, and also Ellie was a really good goalie.)

(And now that she was remembering the

whole thing, Ellie was getting mad all over again.)

"Do you have the bolts?" a voice called out from down below. It was the sort of voice you might expect to hear on television, coming out of a cartoon deer or bunny or talking piece of cake.

"Yep!" Ellie called back, and stuck the two bolts between her lips so her hands were free. She ducked out the door, grabbed hold of the fireman's pole just outside it, and slid down to the ground, sneakers hitting the wood chips with a nice *thud-crunch*.

"Great! What now?" the talking piece of cake said. Only it wasn't a talking piece of cake—it was Kit, Ellie's next-door neighbor, best friend, and future vice president of the engineering company Ellie was going to run one day. (They'd considered being co-presidents, but then Kit decided she really liked being able to call herself VP.) ("VP" stands for "vice president.")

Ellie and Kit were a lot alike. They even had a lot of the same clothes, and they wore them at the same time whenever they could. Today, they were both wearing skirts—but Ellie's was fluffy and purple, and Kit's was smooth and pink. Ellie also had her tool belt strapped snugly around her waist, over her skirt. In it were her most useful tools: a hammer, two screwdrivers, a tape measure, an adjustable wrench, her mini cordless drill (it was an extra-special Christmas present), and—maybe most important of all—a notepad with a little flat pencil. On the back of the notepad she kept a long numbered list of the projects she'd completed. She used the pages inside for sketching brand-new projects.

Ellie reached for the notepad and studied the sketch of today's project. It was a good one.

If it all went according to her plan—which it sometimes did, but sometimes didn't (building was tricky that way)—the water balloon

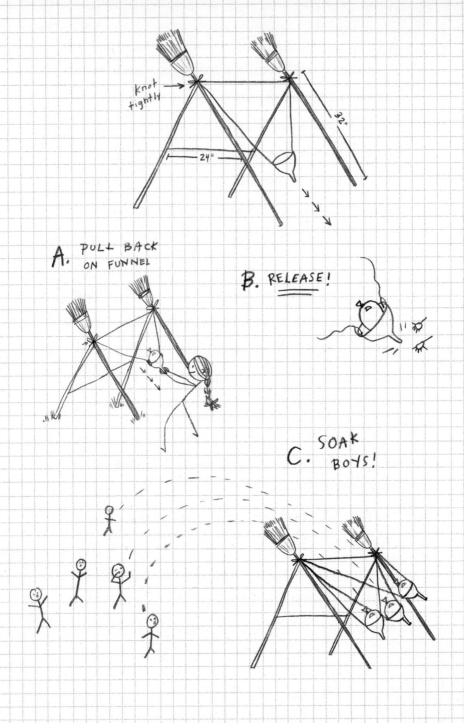

knot
tightly

32"

24"

A. PULL BACK ON FUNNEL

B. RELEASE!

C. SOAK BOYS!

launcher would work like a slingshot and throw water balloons way, way, *way* farther than Ellie and Kit could throw them on their own. To be more specific, it would throw water balloons way, way, way across the yards, right onto the neighborhood boys' heads.

All the mad that Ellie was feeling over the boys' not letting Ellie and Kit play soccer whooshed out of her body, and she rubbed her hands together sneakily. The boys were never going to see this coming!

Ellie pulled her hammer from her tool belt and got to work on the launcher. She nailed brooms together and used a garage sale sign to keep the whole thing nice and solid so it wouldn't tip over when it shot out a balloon.

"Is it time for this?" Kit asked, holding up a funnel and pointing to Ellie's drawing.

"Yep," Ellie said. The funnel was Ellie's dad's—he used it to change the oil in the car. She figured he would understand why she needed to borrow it. Soaking the neighborhood boys for not letting girls play soccer was a pretty good cause.

Ellie pulled down her safety goggles and lifted her drill. She drilled two little holes in each side of the funnel, near the top. The drill was one of her favorite tools because it was the *only* electric tool she was allowed to use without her mom and dad watching. She'd written *Ellie Bell's Drill* across the side in purple paint pen, then drawn some flowers and some dragons, which had mostly rubbed off by now since she used it so much. A drill was a very good tool to have—she could use it to tighten or loosen or put in screws, to put holes in things, and once she'd even attached a fork to the end of it and used it to mix a milk shake. It had worked really well, but her dad said that wasn't an appropriate use of a drill (but then he'd whispered that it was a clever idea all the same).

Ellie looped stretchy exercise bands through the funnel, then tied them to the launcher. Then Kit, who had really good handwriting, wrote *The Water Empress* down one of the broomsticks in fancy swirly letters.

"'Water Empress'?" Ellie asked.

"We can't just call it a water balloon launcher. It has to have a name—like roller coasters and boats."

Ellie nodded—this was the sort of thing Kit was always thinking of.

"It's beautiful," Ellie said, putting her hands on her hips proudly. She smiled—actually, she smirked—then wiggled her fingers anxiously. "Let's get the balloons!"

Chapter Two

They stomped through the soggy part of the yard to the hose, where they filled up twenty-four water balloons. This took a while, since tying balloons was hard, and they ended up getting their shirts and faces and legs soaked (and also making a lot of gross squeaking sounds with the balloons that made them laugh). By the time they were done, they had little bits of grass stuck to their faces, but not even Kit, who didn't much like getting dirty, cared. All they could think about was how surprised and wet and probably mad the boys were going to be, and that was a great thing to think about.

Kit climbed up the ladder to the top of the playhouse, then looked through Ellie's binoculars.

"They're right there! They're still playing soccer in Toby's backyard!" Kit yelled down excitedly.

"All right," Ellie said, bouncing on her toes. "Do they look like they're having fun, without girls playing?"

"Yep," Kit said.

"Do they look dry?"

"I guess Dylan is sort of sweaty, but mostly dry."

"Not for long!" Ellie shouted, which was

really what she'd been waiting to shout the entire time. Then she loaded a big, fat water balloon into the funnel and sat down on the ground. She pulled back hard. So far, so good— the Water Empress felt sturdy!

"Fire!" she shouted, and released the funnel. The balloon shot up into the air, arcing through the sky, whizzing down, and then—

"What happened? Did it get them?" she called up to Kit excitedly.

"No," Kit said, sounding disappointed. "It landed in Ms. Smith's yard. It needs to go farther!"

"Farther." Ellie frowned. She couldn't really pull it back any harder. But she *could* aim it better so it went farther *out* instead of *up*.

"Hurry! I think they're about to go inside for Popsicles!" Kit said urgently.

"Fire!" Ellie yelled, and the balloon soared—but this time, not *up*, *up*, *up* but *out, out, out.* It whizzed across the top of the fence and—

SPLOOSH.

"That's it! You got Dylan right in his dumb face! More, more, more!" Kit yelled, her voice squeaky and especially cakelike.

Ellie put another balloon in the launcher, and another and another. Kit slid down the fireman's pole. She handed Ellie balloons so they could work faster. *SPLOOSH! SPLOOSH! SPLOOSH!* They laughed and screamed and dropped a few balloons, which exploded on the ground, and they could hear the boys yelling and shouting. They were coming to Ellie's house! Kit and Ellie grabbed hold of all the extra balloons and raced back up into the workshop. When the boys busted through the gate, the girls threw the balloons down at them.

"We need water balloons! Find their stockpile!" Dylan said right when a water balloon

SPLOOSHED on his head. His hair flattened in front of his eyes. Ellie and Kit yowled so hard with laughter their eyes watered.

"They took them all to the playhouse!" Toby shouted.

"It's a *workshop*!" Ellie yelled back.

"Get them with the hose!" one of the McClellan boys said, and the other turned the garden hose on—but the blast wasn't strong enough to reach Ellie and Kit up in the workshop. Ellie and Kit dropped to the sawdusty floor while the hose water rained against the side of the workshop, and they high-fived when they heard the McClellan boys give up.

"That's for not letting us play soccer with you!" Ellie yelled.

"I didn't really want to play soccer anyway," Kit whispered.

"Shhhh," Ellie answered.

"This is no fair!" Toby shouted. Even his

voice sounded soggy. "Where did you get a water balloon launcher?"

Ellie laughed loud enough that the sound filled up the whole workshop. "I built it!"

Then she pulled out her notepad and wrote on the back, *Project 61: The Water Empress.*

"*What* happened to the two of you?" Kit's mom asked, horrified. It was half an hour after the epic water balloon fight, and they were standing in the foyer of Kit's house. The foyer had lots of pretend flowers, pictures of Kit, and pictures of Kit holding pretend flowers. Kit had suggested they call for a towel rather than tracking water across the hardwoods, which Ellie thought was very considerate of her. Kit's mother did not seem to recognize this.

"Ellie built a water balloon launcher, and we soaked the boys!" Kit explained excitedly.

"*You're* soaked!"

"But not *as* soaked as they are," Ellie said. Kit's mom narrowed her eyes at Ellie. Kit's mother, like Kit, liked beauty pageants and not getting dirty and ballet class on Tuesdays. Unlike Kit, that was sort of all Kit's mother liked. Because of that, she tended to think that Ellie was a bad influence on Kit. After all, before Ellie, Kit never came home soaking wet! Before Ellie, Kit didn't know how to hammer a nail into the side of the china cabinet! Before Ellie, the blender was in one piece!

(This was not 100 percent Ellie's fault—she didn't know there was a "don't take the appliances apart" rule in Kit's house. Ellie's parents let her take apart appliances, though ever since she took apart the fancy toaster that made perfect toasted bagels, they wanted her to ask permission first.)

(Also, Ellie was the one who encouraged Kit to join the ballet class on Tuesdays because Ellie really loved going to it, and Kit's mother never gave Ellie credit for that.)

"Ugh. Here, here, take these. Can't you two play *nice* games? What about puzzles? A nice, dry puzzle," Kit's mother said, thrusting fancy pink bath towels at both of them.

"I bet I could build a really cool puzzle!" Ellie said, getting excited. She could get some bolts and nuts that fit together, and maybe even make it go up instead of lying flat on a table. She looked at Kit—

"That's not what I meant." Kit's mother jumped in. She then sighed heavily and said, "Why don't you two just go dry off on the back porch in the sun?"

The girls took their fancy pink bath towels outside, and Kit's mother brought them glasses of lemonade. They watched lizards run back and forth on a pile of firewood for a long time, then tried catching a few. Ellie was just starting to draft a lizard-catching device when they heard the phone ring inside. Kit's mother answered it, glanced outside at them, then closed the blinds before she started talking. Obviously, she didn't want them to hear what she had to say.

Which meant it had to be something really good.

Ellie and Kit ran to the kitchen window and crouched under the flower box hanging there. They could hear Kit's mother, but her voice was muffled—they couldn't understand what she was saying.

"Maybe we can sneak the door open just a crack," Ellie said.

"No way. She sees *everything*," Kit answered, looking serious.

"Hmm. Okay. Let's think," Ellie said. She looked around at the back patio, then swished her skirt back and forth, thinking, thinking, thinking . . . "I've got it!" Ellie said. She ran back to the patio table, drank the rest of her lemonade quickly, then held up the glass. "It'll make the sound get to our ears better." She hurried over to the house and put the open part of the glass right up against the outside wall. Then she pressed her ear up to the other end tight-tight-tight so there was no space for the sound to escape.

"Is it working?" Kit asked.

Ellie waited a second . . .

Kit's mother's voice rose through the cup, way louder than before—it worked! "The birthday party will start at four o'clock sharp on Saturday, so we want the special present here by then," she said. Ellie's eyes widened.

"Hurry! She's talking about your birthday!" Ellie whispered. Kit's birthday parties were always amazing. One year her parents

hired real acrobats to come do a show in the front yard. Another year they had horses—not ponies, but real *horses*—come for trail rides. This year Kit was having a birthday tea party, with crumpets and dollops and pastry puffs and other stuff Ellie didn't know anything about but sounded super fancy.

"Woohoo birthday, birthday, birthday!" Kit said, and dumped her lemonade out. She put her glass up against the wall, just like Ellie had.

"Oh, yes, she'll be very excited. She already has a name picked out—Miss Penelope," Kit's mother said on the other side of the wall.

Ellie's eyes widened. So did Kit's. They knew *exactly* what the present was.

Chapter Three

Miss Penelope was Kit's dog—or, at least, what Kit wanted to name a dog if she got one some-day. But Kit was never allowed to have one, since her stepdad and little sister were super allergic to dogs.

"Miss Penelope!" Kit said excitedly.

"Do you really think so?" Ellie asked. "How? Is your family unallergic now?"

"I don't know!" Kit said. Her face was as pink as her skirt. "Miss Penelope! Finally!"

The problem with listening in on people's conversations is that if you learn something really cool—like that you're getting a dog—it's very hard to stay calm. Kit and Ellie ran around the backyard doing cartwheels and round offs and trying to do walkovers but mostly just falling over and rolling down the hill. They were the sort of excited where it felt impossible to stand still.

"I bet we can use the Water Empress to launch tennis balls for Miss Penelope!" Ellie said, rolling down the hill again. She bounced to her feet. "I mean, if she's a big enough dog to catch tennis balls."

"Oh, that's a great idea!" Kit said, only she said it as she was rolling down the hill to meet Ellie, so her words were tumbley. Ellie understood her anyway, of course, because best friends can do things like that. Kit stood up and neatly dabbed the bits of grass from her lips, then went on. "Though . . . what if she doesn't like fetch? Can we build something else for her?"

"Of course!" Ellie said, sitting down cross-legged on the ground. Her skirt was all twisted up around her, but she didn't much care. Kit, however, carefully spread her skirt out before sitting down beside Ellie. "If I'd known you were getting Miss Penelope, I'd have made something for her instead of making you a—" Ellie slapped her hands over her mouth. Kit's face lit up.

Here's why: Ellie *always* built Kit's birth-day present, since it was hard to buy anything good with vacuuming-the-whole-downstairs money. (Everything at the store was so expen-sive, and vacuuming didn't pay very well.) When Kit turned seven, Ellie built her a pair of stilts (Project 14). When Kit turned eight, Ellie built her a skateboard (Project 21). Last year, when Kit turned nine, Ellie built her a desk-size stage with real lights on it so Kit could practice for the Little Miss Auburn-Opelika Pageant (which she won—and which was Project 32, Ellie's biggest one ever at the time).

"What did you build for my present? Tell me!" Kit said, bouncing forward on her knees. "It's okay if I know. If you find out the week of your birthday, it doesn't count as ruining the surprise."

Ellie was almost certain Kit had made up that rule, but Kit was very convincing. Besides, not telling Kit something was hard—Ellie had nearly told her about her present four other times this week and just barely caught herself each time. She took a big breath, then grinned. "Your birthday present is a french-braiding machine! Project sixty, see?" she said, and grabbed her notepad. It was a little soggy from the water balloon fight, so Ellie had to peel the pages apart a bit to show Kit the sketch.

"Ellie! That's amazing! We have to go see

it! Is it done? Is it at your house? It won't count as giving me the present early so long as you don't *give* it to me. We're just looking at it." Kit squealed.

Ellie was pretty sure Kit had made up that rule too, but again, Kit was *very* convincing. "Okay!"

They rushed back over to Ellie's house and up to her bedroom. Ellie was keeping the french-braiding machine under her pillow— Kit would have found it if it'd been in Ellie's workshop. Ellie pulled it out with a big sweep of her arm, like a magician. Kit's eyes went huge and glittery and happy.

"Try it out on me!" Kit said, clapping her hands. "Please, please, please! And then we can both use it before my party and have matching hair!"

Kit sat down in Ellie's desk chair and folded her hands neatly in her lap, like she was at a beauty salon. Ellie pulled Kit's hair behind her ears.

"Madam! Welcome to the *very* lovely, *very* snooty, *very* famous Salon Bell," Ellie said in a funny French voice (or what she thought might be a French voice—she didn't actually know any French people, so she had to guess). Kit giggled. "Now, you are here for a french braid, yes? Lucky for you, this machine will french-braid your hair in no time!"

Ellie split Kit's hair into two pigtails, then looped them through the french braider. She then put her hand on the knob and began to turn it. The braider looped Kit's hair back on itself, back and forth and back and forth, adding a bit more hair here and there and again and—

"Ow," Kit said.

"What?" Ellie said, forgetting to use her French voice.

"It pulled my hair. It's okay, keep going," Kit said, and sat straighter.

Ellie kept turning the knob.

"Ow!" Kit said, louder this time. "That time really hurt! Is it done now?"

Ellie frowned and looked at Kit's head closely. It was sort of hard to tell if it was done. Right now, Kit's head just looked like a big lump of hair with some bits of metal sticking out in a few places. But braids usually looked like that— all messy and crazy and then suddenly at the end, *poof*, they looked great.

"It isn't done yet. Almost," Ellie said nervously, trying to brush aside some of the hair to get a good look at the braid. She went to pull the french braider out of Kit's hair, but—

"Ow, ow, ow! It's pulling my brains out!" Kit said, grabbing the top of her head and pulling away from Ellie. "What's happening back there?"

Ellie cringed. "It's kind of in a big knot right now. All of it. The braider. Your hair. Everything is all knotty."

"What?" Kit said. She sounded like a talking piece of cake again, all high and squeaky. Ellie and Kit tugged and pulled and tried to sort out Kit's hair from the french braider. It wasn't working, not one bit.

"It *does* look like your hair is french braided underneath the knots, though," Ellie said as they walked downstairs to find Ellie's mom and ask for her help.

Kit didn't answer. Ellie didn't blame her.

"Mom? Can you help with something really quick?" Ellie called into her mom's home office.

"I'm working right now, Ellie. Is it a real emergency, or is it a *situation*?" Ellie's mom asked without looking over. This was something Ellie's mom had discussed with Ellie a number of times. Real *emergencies* involved blood, bones, explosions, fires, floods, the car, and the good hedge clippers. Anything else was a *situation* and could wait until Ellie's mom wasn't working.

"It's a situation," Ellie said glumly. "Come on, Kit. Maybe we can rub some peanut butter into your hair to unstick it."

"Oh no, you don't!" Ellie's mom shouted, springing to her feet. "What's going on—oh! Kit! Is that a robot in your hair? What is happening?"

"It's a french braider," Kit answered sadly.

"A french knotter, mostly," Ellie said, just as sadly.

Ellie's mom sighed. "Ellie—go get me a good comb and some hair conditioner. Kit, I'm going to call your mother, okay?"

It took approximately one hour, one bottle of conditioner, two globs of butter, a screwdriver, and two grown-ups to get Kit's hair unknotted from the french braider. The screwdriver was because Ellie had to take apart the french braider piece by piece as they picked through Kit's hair (which *was* french braided underneath the knots, Ellie noticed, but she decided not to point this out because Kit's mom was already looking very unhappy about the whole thing).

"There we go! You're free, Kit. And we didn't even have to shave your head!" Ellie's mom joked when they were finished.

"You don't know how afraid I was we'd have to," Kit's mom said not-at-all-jokingly, then turned to look at Ellie. "Young lady, I don't want to see *any* engineering around my daughter's hair ever again, especially just before pageant season! We will *not* be one of those cheaters using wigs to win!" Ellie didn't really see how wigs were cheating, but she decided this was probably a bad time to mention that.

Kit rubbed her head tenderly, then made a face when her fingers came away oily. "It's okay, Mom. It isn't Ellie's fault. Besides, I asked her to try the french braider out on me."

"Well, perhaps Ellie can find someone with shorter hair to engineer with, then," Kit's mom said, gathering her things. "Perhaps give those neighborhood boys a call. They don't mind getting soaked or dirty or having oily hair. Now, Kit, let's get home—we absolutely have to wash that butter out of your hair."

What a wreck of a birthday present! Ellie thought, slomping up to her room after Kit and her mom were gone. Plus, since she'd had to take the french braider apart, now she had nothing for Kit's birthday present on Saturday. How had this day gone from Water Empress to Miss Penelope to capital-"D" Disaster so quickly? She pulled out her notebook, drew a giant sad face over *Project 60: French Braider*, and then flipped to a new page. It'd taken ages and ages to come up with the french braider, and now Ellie only had a few days before the party to come up with and build a whole new project. But would Kit even *want* a new present from Ellie now?

She won't if it has anything to do with her hair, Ellie thought, doodling some gears on the blank sheet of paper. She wondered if maybe her mom would take her to the store to buy a regular present, like a toy or some of those really nice markers that come in weird colors. Maybe a pretty collar for Miss Penelope. Or a Frisbee! Or—

Ellie's fingers got jittery, which happened a lot when she was getting an idea for a new project—it was like her fingers were just as excited as her heart. Why buy Miss Penelope a present when Ellie could build one herself? A present that would *not* get caught in anyone's hair, require any butter or water balloons, or make Kit's mom give Ellie a *look*. It was perfect, better even than the french braider would have been.

Ellie would build the world's best doghouse for Miss Penelope!

Chapter Four

The next day, Ellie woke up super early. She wanted to check out other doghouses in the neighborhood for ideas, but also, she was doing her weekly Fix-It Walk. Every Tuesday in the summer, she walked around the neighborhood to make sure there was nothing that needed touching up or nailing or tightening or repairing. She snapped her tool belt on over her favorite sundress (pink with crisscross straps and beads), then pulled down her sunglasses. It was so early that the neighborhood was all misty and foggy and cool. It *had* to be this early—she needed to make sure she got out before Kit saw her, since obviously she wouldn't be able to invite Kit along. It was a surprise present, after all.

Ellie took a right out her front door and started down the block. Her tool belt made a satisfying *jingle-thud* noise as she walked. She stopped just outside the Millers' house. They had a dog—and a doghouse. She peered through the fence to get a better look.

"Are you investigating them?" a voice said behind her. She spun around so fast that one of her screwdrivers fell out of her belt. It was Toby Michaels, standing there with his arms folded and chin up. He said, "Because if you're going to investigate, you need an investigating hat. Like Sherlock Holmes has."

"You don't *need* that to investigate. It's just

the hat a famous investigator wears," Ellie pointed out, picking up her screwdriver.

"So you *are* investigating them?"

"No."

"Are you robbing them? That is called 'casing the joint.' If you're robbing them. It's what you do before you rob. You 'case.'"

"I'm not robbing them! Do I look like a robber?"

"I don't know. I've never seen a robber—"

"Toby Michaels, I'm researching doghouses," Ellie snapped. "I'm building one as a surprise present for Kit. Which I shouldn't have told you, since now you have to keep it a secret too. Promise you won't tell her?"

Toby shrugged. "Sure. But you're the one who's always telling Kit secrets, you know."

Ellie made a face at him, then looked back through the fence. The Millers' doghouse wasn't very interesting, but it did have a nice little border around the door. She sketched it quickly in her notepad, thinking about what sort of wood she'd need to use for that. Maybe instead of wood, she could put some nails around the door and then string ribbons . . .

"You're drawing their doghouse?" Toby asked.

Ellie sighed. "I'm *researching* doghouses. It's important to research before you build something."

Toby's mouth widened a bit. When he did this, she could see he was missing one of his back teeth. It must have just fallen out, because there wasn't even a little bit of the new tooth showing. "So you're going to *build* a doghouse. Like you built that water balloon launcher?"

"Exactly. I'm an engineer," Ellie said.

"Like the kind that drives a train?" Toby asked, eyebrow raised.

"No, like the kind that builds things and

knows about wires and electricity and construction and stuff like that—like my dad," Ellie said. "Or, at least, I'm going to be an engineer someday. So I'm practicing now."

"Oh, cool," he said. "So, can I help research the doghouses?"

"I thought you didn't like playing with girls. You wouldn't let us play soccer with you yesterday," Ellie said, folding her arms and lifting her eyebrows, just like her mom did whenever Ellie was in trouble.

Toby kicked at the ground a little. He didn't say anything. If you knew Toby Michaels, you'd know what a big deal that was. Toby Michaels was the sort of kid who *always* had something to say.

Ellie waited.

Finally, Toby said, "We should've let you guys play. Dylan was a really bad goalie anyway."

"Uh-huh," Ellie said.

"Sorry." He sounded like he really was sorry. And sort of embarrassed.

"Uh-huh," Ellie said.

"So . . . can I help research the doghouses? I know all the neighbors, and their pets. It'll go faster if I help. And then maybe in exchange, you can show me how you build the doghouse. I've never built anything before."

Ellie fiddled with the top of her hammer, spinning it around in its loop. She didn't want to tell him no if he really did want to learn about building things. After all, she really loved engineering—it was fun to share that with people. Even Toby Michaels-type people.

Besides, if he was a jerk boy about it, she'd just soak him again.

"Okay," she said. "Let's go."

Now the *jingle-thud* noise of her tool belt was punctuated by the slap of Toby's flip-flops on the ground. They came to another backyard.

"Don't bother. They don't have a doghouse. The man who lives here is an executive. See the car? Executives have nice cars—"

"We're not researching doghouses in this yard," Ellie said, cutting him off. "I'm going to fix the mailbox." She pointed at the mailbox. The screw that held in the little flag had come loose; the flag was hanging limply, pointing to the ground. She looked closely at the screw holding the flag in, then chose a screwdriver from her tool belt.

"Why that one?" Toby asked, pointing at the other screwdriver she had.

"This is a flathead screw," Ellie said, showing him. The top of the screw had one line right down the middle. "So I have to use the flathead screwdriver. The other screwdriver is called a Phillips head—it's for screws that have a little plus-sign shape on the top."

"Huh," Toby said. "Who is Phillips?"

Ellie shrugged. She carefully put the screwdriver into the screw and turned it to the right. The flag tightened right back up. She stepped back to admire her work, then moved on.

They saw three more doghouses. Toby knew just where to look, like he promised. One doghouse had a tiled roof. Another was really two doghouses in one. The last one had a single slanted roof instead of a triangle one. You couldn't really see it from the road, but luckily, Toby knew the owner of the house. Toby seemed to know everybody. He'd knock on the door, and they'd say, "Good morning, Toby!" like he was the best thing to come around since the sun that morning. He even shook their hands, like an adult.

Ellie was impressed.

"So, where are you going to build this doghouse?" Toby asked as Ellie finished up drawing the one with the slanted roof.

"Well, it won't fit in my workshop. I guess in the backyard near the tire swing? That's where I build bigger projects," she explained.

"But won't Kit see it, since she lives right next door?"

Ellie frowned. She'd been so focused on designing and building the doghouse that she'd sort of forgotten about this. Sometimes, her parents let her build in the garage, but it wasn't much fun and it always smelled like lawnmowers.

"I have an idea," Toby said. "You can build it in my yard. My parents won't care. And I promise not to mess with it when you aren't there."

Ellie thought about this as she walked toward the next fence. There was a big doghouse in the backyard, one with a domed roof and a little built-in trough—for food, Ellie guessed. She began to draw it.

"What's going on out here?" a voice asked.

The lady who owned the house was standing at the door, looking confused. "Who are you?"

"Oh—hello. I'm Ellie, neighborhood engineer. I was just drawing your doghouse," Ellie said, feeling a little worried about the look on the lady's face—it wasn't a mean look, but it wasn't a friendly look either.

"Mrs. Carter! You look great this morning. Is that a new haircut?" Toby said warmly, and then he shook her hand. "Listen—didn't you have someone come work on your deck last week? Is there maybe some wood left over that Ellie could have? She's building a doghouse."

"Oh!" Mrs. Carter said. "You know, I think there is. Just go around back and grab whatever you see."

Toby gave Ellie a look that said, *See? I'm helpful!*

He had a point. Ellie let herself and Toby in through the side gate and started toward the pile of wood, which was near the doghouse

Ellie had just been drawing. There were some really good pieces! They gathered them up and started back toward the gate.

"Muffintop!" Mrs. Carter shouted, startling both of them.

This was a very weird thing for someone to yell for no reason. But when Ellie looked, she realized that Mrs. Carter actually had a very good reason for shouting, "Muffintop!" It was the name of her fluffy black-and-white dog. The dog that had just jetted out through the gate Ellie had left open.

Chapter Five

Ellie and Toby dropped all the wood in their arms and sprinted for the gate. *Where did that dog even come from?* Ellie wondered as Muffintop sidestepped and sniffed and stopped to pee on some flowers.

"Muffintop! Here, boy! Come back!" Ellie called. Toby whistled loudly. Mrs. Carter tried shouting tricks: "Come back, Muffintop, and we'll go get a treat!"

Muffintop was not fooled. He pranced back and forth outside the gate, then turned and ran, pink tongue lolling out of his mouth, grinning toothily like this was the *best day ever*.

"You have to catch him!" Mrs. Carter said to Ellie and Toby, looking frantic. "He never stops running if you don't catch him!"

Ellie dashed after Muffintop. Toby was right behind her, trying to whistle and run at the same time.

"Border collies are known for being an extremely high-energy breed of dog!" he said, panting.

"No kidding," Ellie called back.

Muffintop dashed down the street, looking over his shoulder to see if they were still chasing him. When he saw they were, he cut hard to the side and darted around a flowerbed, then a house, then—

"Look out!" Ellie called, but it was no use.

Muffintop dove into a rack of clothes that some-one was just wheeling out for a garage sale. The garage sale lady screamed and flailed her hands around, but it was too late to stop the dog. Muffintop barked and emerged from the other side of the clothes with a pair of flowery pants wrapped around his neck like a scarf. His pants-scarf fluttered as he leaped into the air, clearing a table of Santa figurines, only to crash-land into a pile of books.

Muffintop clambered to his feet, upsetting the neat piles of books. He was still wearing the pants-scarf. He shook, and hair went every-where. Muffintop looked pretty happy about this. He drooled on the nearest book.

"Get out of here, dog!" the garage sale lady shouted, brandishing a broom in Muffintop's direction.

Muffintop leaped to the side, like he thought even this angry lady was just playing a game with him. The lady swung the broom again and again, and Muffintop nearly backflipped in delight. Then, he started running again.

Ellie threw her hands in the air. "Ugh. We're never going to catch him like this!"

"What if we had help?" Toby asked as they watched Muffintop stop and snatch the tomatoes off one of their neighbor's bushes with his teeth. He crunched each of them, like he expected the tomatoes to be toy balls; when they smashed in his mouth, he spit them out, then tried another and another and another.

"Help would be good. I could go get Kit," Ellie said.

"You and Kit live on the other end of the neighborhood—Dylan and the McClellan twins live right there! I'll go get them," Toby said, and sprinted away before Ellie could argue.

The neighborhood boys? Hanging out with Toby was one thing, but Ellie didn't really want to hang out with the rest of them.

It's not just hanging out—it's work! You're trying to catch that dog, she reminded herself. And, if it was work, that meant she probably should see if there was anything she could build to catch Muffintop faster.

"Excuse me," she said to the garage sale lady, who was picking up the clothing that had been knocked to the ground. "I'd like to buy this." Ellie held up a water-ski rope.

"That's a quarter," the lady said.

"I'm going to use it to catch that dog," Ellie explained.

"That's free, then," the lady said, looking huffy. Ellie took off running with the rope—but not toward Toby and the neighborhood boys he'd gathered, and not toward Muffintop.

"Where are you going?" Toby shouted across the lawns.

"Chase him toward your backyard!" she shouted to Toby. "And bring a snack!"

"But my backyard doesn't have a fence!

And what kind of snack?" Toby yelled, but Ellie didn't answer. She had to beat the boys and Muffintop to Toby's backyard, and fast. She ran through the yards, dress and tool belt and water-ski rope flailing out behind her, kicking up newly mowed grass. She slid into Toby's backyard. There was the soccer goal the boys had been using yesterday. There was no time to sketch this project out, so she just had to imagine the way she'd draw it.

Ellie scrambled up a tree (she was basically an expert tree climber). It was another minute or two before she heard Muffintop's barking and the neighborhood boys' shouting. They were coming! Ellie crouched low and watched Muffintop dash by underneath her. He was still wearing his pants-scarf. Ellie wondered if the garage sale lady would want it back.

"Psssst!" she whispered when Toby and the boys walked underneath her tree. They looked up, confused. "Did you bring a snack?" she asked Toby.

Dylan held up a bag of potato chips.

"Perfect," Ellie said. "Open them and sprinkle them in the soccer goal."

"Huh?" Dylan asked.

"Just do it!" Toby told him. Dylan darted forward and tore open the bag of chips. Muffintop, who was disappointed no one was chasing him, was sniffing around the back of Toby's yard.

"Aw, man. I thought we were going to eat them," one of the McClellan twins said as the chips fell to the ground.

"Now what?" Toby asked as Dylan returned.

"Stand back," Ellie said. The neighborhood boys and Toby looked a little confused, but they stepped back. Muffintop sniffed closer and closer and closer to the soccer goal. Then a gentle breeze blew, and Muffintop caught the scent of the potato chips. He sniffed at the air, then followed his nose to the goal. There, he lowered his tomato-stained snout to the ground and began to happily crunch up all the chips, tail wagging.

"I bet they're really good," a McClellan said, pouting.

"Almost . . . almost . . . ," Ellie muttered to herself. *There!* She pulled hard on the water-ski rope. The rope snapped tight, pulled round the deck, across the lawn, to the goal. The goal fell over! Muffintop was trapped inside.

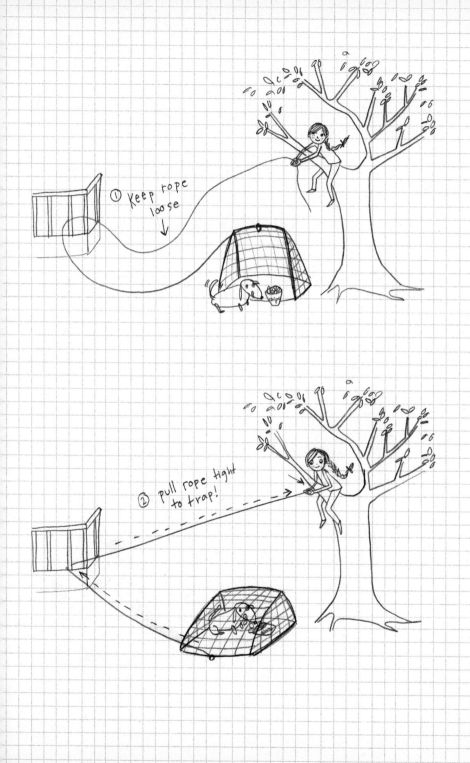

Chapter Six

"Wherever did he acquire a pair of pants?" Mrs. Carter asked when they brought Muffintop back to her.

"It's sort of a long story," Toby said. "But here he is! Sorry about that, Mrs. Carter."

"Thank you all for bringing him back. Come along now, Muffintop—is that a potato chip stuck to your fur?" Mrs. Carter said, hauling Muffintop inside by the collar.

"Wait, wait—Mrs. Carter, can we still have some of that wood we were getting? You know, before Muffintop got out? For Ellie's doghouse?" Toby said.

"Oh!" Mrs. Carter said. "Yes, yes. Of course. Just go around back and grab whatever you see. I'll keep Muffintop inside this time, just to be safe."

"A doghouse?" one of the boys asked as soon as Mrs. Carter shut the door.

"Yep," Toby said. "Ellie's building one. She's *really* good at building stuff."

"I'm an engineer," Ellie explained.

"Isn't that the person who drives the train?" Dylan asked.

"That's a different sort of engineer," Ellie said.

"Can we help?" the McClellan twins asked.

Ellie frowned. This was turning into a big project, with so many people wanting to help. Plus, she wasn't so sure she trusted the neighborhood boys when they were all together like this. Boys, as far as she could tell, were sort of like rabbits. One was fine and maybe even interesting to play with, but a whole bunch of them would just be a lot of jumping and running and smelling. Plus, if they—the boys, not the rabbits—started being jerks again, she'd have to fight with them or, worse, start over on her own with the doghouse.

"How about I promise to come get you if we need help?" Ellie asked. "And we might. This is a big project."

Dylan and the McClellan twins were kind of disappointed, but they agreed and went back to their houses. Meanwhile, Ellie and Toby gathered up all the spare deck wood that they'd thrown to the ground when the Muffintop chase began. They carried it back to Toby's backyard and dropped it in the grass.

Toby watched as Ellie drew her doghouse plans. She wanted to use the best parts of all the doghouses she'd studied that day. The shingles on the roof from one. The little deck on the side from another. The border around the door, and the tiny ramp, and maybe the window on one side.

"Wow. Will it look just like that? Because that looks really good," Toby said.

"Mostly. Sometimes you have to make stuff up on the spot when you're engineering," Ellie explained.

"That's called *improvising*," Toby said, and Ellie was getting so used to him being a know-it-all that she didn't even think about rolling her eyes at him.

Ellie left Toby to sort out the wood they'd collected as she hurried to the workshop, thinking through all the stuff they'd need along the way. A saw (not the electric one, since she

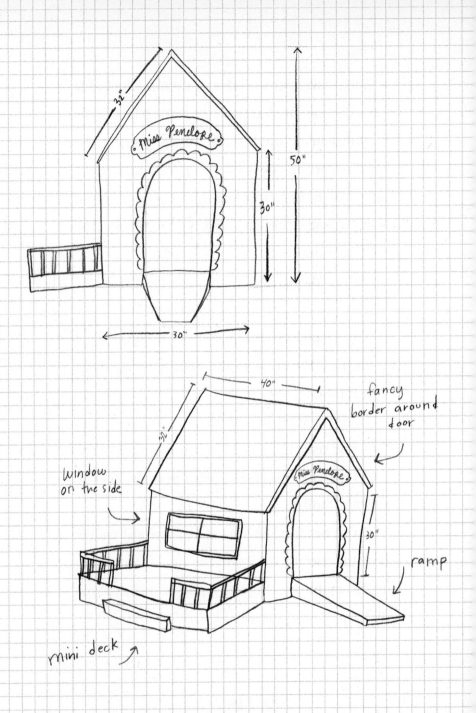

32"

Miss Penelope

50"

30"

30"

40"

fancy border around door

32"

window on the side

Miss Penelope

30"

ramp

mini deck

wasn't allowed to use that without an adult), a level, some more nails, her builder's square (which wasn't a square at all—it was a triangle—so it was sort of a weird name). By the time she got everything and made it back to Toby's house, she saw that he was drinking an orange soda, standing over the spare wood from Mrs. Carter. He'd sorted it into piles according to length.

"It's important to stay organized," Toby explained. "People who are organized are way more efficient than people who aren't. If you'd been longer, I'd have color coded them—that's when you assign a color to each piece."

"Right," Ellie said. She laid down the sketch of the doghouse so she could see it. First things first—the bottom. She'd start there and build up to the roof.

She grabbed a big flat piece of wood from Toby's pile—that would be a good floor. She nailed a couple of smaller pieces of wood onto the bottom side as a base, so that it wasn't just sitting flat on the ground. This way water wouldn't soak into Miss Penelope's house through the dirt. Then she began nailing in pieces for the walls.

"Did you take a special class in engineering? Does it meet every week? My karate class meets every week. So if engineering class is on Thursdays, I can't go," Toby said, watching.

Ellie shook her head. "You don't need a special class to build things. Maybe to build really big things, like skyscrapers or lasers, but you can build things just for fun."

"What happens if they don't work?"

"You build something new," Ellie said, shrugging. "Just like how sometimes you have to use a whole bunch of construction paper before you make a really good drawing." She stuck her pencil behind her ear. "We need something for this wall—we won't have enough wood. And something for the roof, since we don't have shingles. Something waterproof . . ." Ellie thought for a moment. What was waterproof? The big thick leaves off the magnolia trees, but they would probably crumble up eventually. Plastic bags, but that wasn't very pretty, and Miss Penelope was probably going to be a very pretty sort of dog. Metal, but where would she find a bunch of metal? She turned to Toby—

"That's it!" she said, and grabbed the orange soda from his hand. "Do you have more of these?"

"I'm only allowed one per day," Toby said.

"More cans, I mean," Ellie explained.

Toby led her to the recycling bin, which was full of orange soda cans. He finished the can he was drinking and tossed it in with the others. "What do we need a bunch of old cans for?"

"Not cans," Ellie said. "*Shingles*."

"Those are cans."

"But they'll be shingles for us."

"But they're cans—"

"Toby!" Ellie said impatiently. "Do you want to learn how to build things or not? Sometimes you have to improvise. I used exercise bands on the water balloon launcher, and those worked just fine for soaking you, didn't they?"

Toby nodded, remembering. "Okay. How many cans do we need?"

"Bunches. And some sharp scissors."

She and Toby carefully cut the cans in half, then flattened them by jumping up and down on them. It took the rest of the morning and some of the afternoon too—Ellie really wished she could ask Kit to come help and make it all go faster, but of course, she couldn't. When they were finally done, they had almost a hundred flat orange soda cans. Ellie nailed them onto the roof one by one.

"Here's a problem, though," Ellie said as they stood back and admired their work. "It needs to be fancy."

"It's already awfully fancy," Toby said, nodding toward the soda-can shingles.

"No, I mean *pretty* fancy. You know. With flowers and sparkles and stuff—fancy like Kit is."

"Oh! Right." Toby frowned. "I might have some stickers we could put on the walls. They have scratch-n-sniff hotdogs on them."

"I don't really think hotdog-smelling stickers are Kit's sort of fancy. That's nice of you to offer though," Ellie said politely.

Toby shrugged, like he couldn't see why anyone wouldn't be interested in hotdog-scented stickers.

"Normally," Ellie went on quickly, "I'd ask

Kit to do the fancying. She's good at drawing and putting stripes and paint and cushions on stuff. But I can't do that since it's a surprise."

"Maybe we could trace something," Toby suggested. "Like trace our hands to make turkeys."

"Turkeys are nice, but I really wanted the big part to have flowers on the wall, like in Kit's bedroom."

"I can't draw flowers," Toby said.

"Me neither," Ellie answered. She thought for a moment—who did she know, other than Kit, who could draw?

Of course. Ellie couldn't believe she hadn't thought of this before!

She turned to Toby. "I think I might have an idea. I'll go work on that, and maybe we can meet up tomorrow to keep working?"

"Good," Toby said, standing up and dusting off his hands. "Engineering really takes it out of you. Tomorrow maybe we should bring snacks. It's good for your blood sugar to eat snacks."

"Sure—I'll bring snacks. See you tomorrow!" she said, then took off at a run.

Chapter Seven

It was late in the afternoon, the part of the day where the sun wasn't burning you up but the air was still fat and heavy. Ellie cut around the neighborhood, through the school playground and along the fence to a house with a fancy front porch and a swimming pool in the back. There was nothing on it that needed fixing, even though if it had been Ellie's, she probably would have built a pulley to bring the mail right up to the front porch, since the hill it sat on was really steep and sort of a pain to walk up.

The house belonged to McKinley Caplan (or, technically, to her parents), but Ellie knew McKinley would have her two best friends, Madison and Taylor, over—they were basically always together in the summer, sort of like Ellie and Kit. Madison, Taylor, and McKinley were also in Mrs. Funderburk's class, but they were the kind of girls Ellie was mostly friends with only at school. There was nothing *wrong* with them—they were perfectly nice, and they always went to each other's birthday and pool parties—it was just that they didn't have so much in common during the summer, when school was out. Madison, Taylor, and McKinley drew and made their own comic book, called *The Presidents* since their names were also the names of presidents of the United States (the characters in the comic were superhero president versions of themselves). Ellie liked to read their comic books, but she had trouble sitting still for as long as it took to draw one on her own. Besides, Ellie wasn't the name of any president so far, so it'd mess up the title.

McKinley answered the door when Ellie knocked. "Guys, Ellie Bell's here!" she called back toward the kitchen, and Madison and Taylor hurried down the hall.

"Hi," Ellie said to all of them. "I know you're probably working on a comic, so I'll be super quick. Remember how I'm an engineer?"

"Really? Oh! Wait! I remember! You brought that hammer to class last year and got in trouble!" McKinley said brightly.

"Wait, what? I wasn't in your class last

year," Madison said, looking between the two of them.

Ellie sighed. "I brought a hammer for show-and-tell."

"And hammers aren't allowed?" Madison asked.

"The hammer was okay, I guess, but what really got me in trouble was nailing something into the teacher's desk. It was just a tiny little nail, and it popped right out. I was only trying to do a *demonstration*."

"It was the coolest show-and-tell, even though she got a note sent home," McKinley assured Madison and Taylor. This made Ellie grin.

"Well, anyway—I'm an engineer, and I'm building something for Kit's birthday party on Saturday, and wanted to see if you could help with part of it." She reached into her tool belt for her notebook, then flipped it open to show them the sketch of Miss Penelope's house. The girls clustered around it. They looked impressed.

"What do you need help with?" Madison asked.

"I thought it'd be nice to put wallpaper inside, like the flowery stuff in Kit's bedroom. You know, so it matches? But I can't draw flowers. Normally I'd ask Kit, but since it's a present for her . . ."

"Oh!" Madison said. "I think we can do that. If we have enough construction paper."

"I know where the emergency school-supply drawer is," McKinley said. "We can raid it if we need extra. We can do this in no time. Can you leave the sketch with us, so we know about how many flowers we need to draw to cover the walls?"

"Oh, hmm," Ellie said, looking at the sketch. "I would, but we need this one for the build."

"*We?*" McKinley asked. "Who's helping you?"

Ellie bit her lip. The Presidents didn't get along with the neighborhood boys—Toby included. Sometimes the boys made fun of the comic book, and other times The Presidents made fun of how much the boys liked soccer. Ellie wasn't so sure she should tell them Toby was helping her build the doghouse—The Presidents might not want to help anymore, or maybe they'd be mad or grossed out or think Ellie only wanted to play with the boys now. It'd probably be easier, she decided, to just not say anything about Toby.

"Oh, I just meant *we* like you three and me, that's all," she said.

"Oh! Well, we can just draw lots and lots of flowers to be sure there's enough. Besides, you can never have too many spare flowers," Madison said. "This is such a cool present."

"Yep," Ellie said. "Kit is going to love it!"

"Oh! Ellie! I didn't know you were over here," a grown-up voice said. It was Mrs. Caplan, McKinley's mom. "I heard a rumor about you, Miss Bell. Is it true you launched water balloons at all those boys yesterday?"

"You did *what?*" Taylor asked.

"It's true," Ellie said, not sure if she was in trouble with Mrs. Caplan or not.

Mrs. Caplan smiled. "That sounds like it was a lot of fun. Though you aren't here to build another water balloon launcher, are you?"

"No, Mrs. Caplan," Ellie said.

"But *can* she?" McKinley asked. "*Please*, Mom? We never get to soak the boys! And they always deserve it."

"Maybe another day," Mrs. Caplan said. "You kids have fun! And put my good scissors back where you found them, McKinley. I know you've been using them."

"Sorry, Mom!" McKinley said, while Taylor and Madison giggled. McKinley turned back to Ellie. "Those boys are so gross. I'm glad you soaked them. They've been playing Ding Dong Ditch over here all week because they *know* we're on a deadline with this week's comic book."

Ding Dong Ditch was a pretty stupid game, if you asked Ellie—you ran up, rang someone's doorbell, then ran away. Where was the fun in that? Making someone answer their door? Ellie had never understood it, but the neighborhood boys played it every summer all the same. They never got in trouble either, since they'd each say someone else did the actual ding-donging. Ellie supposed Toby was missing the game since he was helping out with the doghouse, and she wondered if The Presidents might like him if they knew that.

"Can you build something that will throw

those boys off the porch when they try to ring the bell? Like a giant spring that *boings* them away?" Taylor said, rubbing her fingers together at the thought.

"That's probably pretty dangerous. And I don't know where to get a spring that big," Ellie said, considering it. "But I have an idea. Not to stop them, but to catch them. I bet if one of them gets in trouble, the others will stop."

"Okay, but I'm going to look up how to buy giant springs later, just in case," Taylor said seriously.

Ellie turned to a new page in her notepad and waved her hand over it, thinking. "Hmm. I think I have an idea. But do you have any red paint?"

"I have red paint powder. You mix it with water to make the paint," McKinley said.

"The powder is even better! Now, if we can

just find an empty ketchup bottle . . . ," Ellie said, and began to sketch out the build.

When a boy ran up and rang the doorbell, stepping on the mat would cause the ketchup bottle under the mat to squeeze. That would send a big whoosh of air down the tube, which would send a poof of red paint powder up at him. The Ding-Dong-Ditcher would get coated— he'd be caught red-handed and red-faced and red-bodied! Since things hadn't gone so well with Kit's mom the day before, Ellie decided they should show Mrs. Caplan the build, just in case.

"Red paint powder?" Mrs. Caplan asked curiously.

"Mom, it's *such* a good idea. Then after they ring today you can just call all their moms and ask who has a red hand, and then they'll get in trouble and the doorbell will *stop ringing*," McKinley said, looking dire.

boy foot

↓ tube

paint powder

empty ketchup bottle

foot presses down

air whooshes

paint powder explosion!

"I do like the idea of the doorbell not ringing," Mrs. Caplan said, nodding. "All right, go
ahead. If anyone gets electrocuted, please
come find me, okay? I'll be in the kitchen,
starting the tacos."

It took no time at all to put together the
door alarm. Ellie found a bike tire tube in
the garage, and they used cardboard paper
towel rolls to load up the paint. McKinley badly
wanted to test the alarm out when they were
finished, but Taylor and Madison talked her
out of it—they had a comic to finish *and* flowers to draw, after all.

"Thanks, Ellie!" Madison said, waving as
Ellie walked back down the driveway.

"Thank you guys," Ellie called back.

"We'll call you if we catch one of those jerk
boys!" McKinley added gleefully.

Ellie gave them a thumbs-up, but the truth
was, she felt a little bad. The boys had helped

her catch that dog, after all, and Toby was being especially helpful. How much trouble would they get in for playing Ding Dong Ditch and coming home covered in paint powder?

Chapter Eight

Ellie went straight to her workshop when she arrived home so she could put away her tools—as much as she loved building, she was ready to take a break for the rest of the afternoon. She hung her tool belt on a hook by the door and carefully put her heaviest tools—like her hammer—in their spots on a shelf. Her workshop might look like chaos to some people, but

Ellie knew exactly where everything was. This was important—if something went wrong with a build, you didn't want to be stuck digging for the right sort of screwdriver or bolt. When everything was put away, she started back down the ladder.

"Ellie! Where have you been?" Kit asked. Ellie jumped, startled. Kit was standing on her side of the fence, but she had a clear view of Ellie climbing down from the workshop. Kit waved.

"Oh! I just had to do . . . errands," Ellie said.

Kit gave Ellie a long look, her head tilted to one side. Kit *always* knew when Ellie was lying—best friends were just like that. "Errands?"

"Your hair doesn't look oily anymore!" Ellie said, changing the subject.

"I had to take three showers. Hey, want to come run through the sprinkler with me? Mom's about to put it out," Kit said.

The truth was, Ellie was *tired*, even though it wasn't even dinnertime yet. But she couldn't just turn down the chance to run through the sprinkler with Kit. It was one of their favorite summer games.

"Yes! Let me go put on my bathing suit," Ellie said. She grabbed another rung of her treehouse ladder and was about to pop out of sight when Kit said something that made Ellie freeze right there.

"Do you want to invite Toby?" she asked. Kit's voice was very careful, like she was testing something.

"Why would I want to invite Toby?" Ellie asked quickly, shaking her head like this was just bonkers.

"Weren't you playing with him earlier? My mom said she saw you and Toby chasing a dog with some pants. I didn't really know if she meant the dog was wearing the pants or you were chasing the dog *with* some pants, though,"

Kit said, putting a finger to her lips thought-fully as she said this.

"That wasn't playing. We were both just trying to catch the dog, that's all," Ellie said.

"Okay. I wondered why you didn't invite me to chase a dog wearing pants," Kit answered. "I thought maybe you were mad we had to break the french braider to get my hair out."

"No, no. That's not it. I promise," Ellie said. "Let me go put my bathing suit on and we'll sprinkler, okay?"

Ellie supposed she could have let Kit invite Toby to play in the sprinkler. But what if Toby said something about the doghouse? Or what if Toby made fun of their sprinkler game? Or what if Toby was a jerk boy, or what if Kit didn't want to play with a boy, or what if . . . ?

There were just an awful lot of what-ifs, and it seemed easier to just not tell Kit about Toby at all.

Kit and Ellie ran through the sprinkler together until the ground was so soggy their feet sank down deep into the grass and made sucking noises when they pulled their toes free. Then, they started their very favorite sprinkler game—one of them would lie down right on top of the sprinkler, which tickled like crazy. Whoever could stand it longest won. Ellie went first.

"I wonder if Miss Penelope will like water. Some dogs don't, you know," Kit said, using her fingers to keep track of the seconds.

"She probably will, since—*hee-hee-hee*—you do!" Ellie said, trying hard to keep from giggling when the sprayer went right over her belly button. She stayed on the sprinkler though, so Kit kept counting.

"Maybe she'll run through the sprinkler with us! That would be so much fun, wouldn't it?" Kit asked.

Ellie didn't say anything, mostly because she was trying too hard to stay on the sprinkler while it tickled her, but also because she was worried that if she talked about Miss Penelope, she'd accidentally spill the beans about the doghouse. She'd already told Kit about her first birthday present, after all. "Ah! I can't take it! How many seconds did I get?" Ellie said, springing away from the sprinkler.

"Twenty-four. My turn!" Kit said, and splashed down onto the sprinkler. Unlike Ellie, Kit was very careful to keep her face from getting mud specks on it. Kit managed twenty-eight seconds of being tickled, which wasn't quite a record but was close. Eventually, Kit's mom came out and put the sprinkler away, smiling a little hard at Ellie as she did so.

"I thought you might be off playing with those boys again," Kit's mom said. "It looked like you were having fun."

"Oh, no. Not at all. Just catching that loose dog," Ellie said fast. *Too* fast. Kit tilted her head to the side again, and Ellie felt her cheeks heat up. "I think I need to go home and take a bath before dinner though. Bye, Kit! See you tomorrow!"

"I hope so!" Kit called after her, sounding a little sad. Ellie almost, *almost* turned around—because it was absolutely nuts for Kit to say that. After all, it was summer vacation! Kit and Ellie saw each other *every day* during summer vacation.

Well. They wouldn't have today, technically, if Kit hadn't seen Ellie climbing down from the workshop. Ellie was too busy working on a project with Toby and The Presidents. Working on a project *without* Kit.

It'll be okay—it's all for Kit's party. Once Kit sees why I've been sneaky, she'll understand, thought Ellie. *Right?*

Chapter Nine

Ellie couldn't help waking up early the next morning—it was so exciting to be in the middle of a build. She snuck out the front door so Kit wouldn't see her leave, then ran down the street to Toby's house. He was already awake and in the backyard, with the doghouse, which made Ellie happy. She bet he was as excited about the build as she was. Ellie walked up and noticed he was drinking an orange soda and writing something on a notepad.

"Isn't it early to be drinking your soda for the day?" Ellie said, pointing to the can. She was only teasing, but Toby jumped, then scrambled to hide the notepad.

"Oh, this is an old can. It's just water inside," he said quickly, pouring out a tiny bit from the soda can to prove it. "If you put water in once you're done, it still tastes a little orange soda-y."

"What were you drawing?" Ellie asked. She walked over and sat down beside him on the deck steps, but Toby kept leaning back and forward to keep her from seeing his notepad.

"It's nothing. Come on, let's keep building! Did you find someone to do the flowers?"

"Yep. I have some connections," she said.

This got Toby's attention. His eyebrows went up a little. "You have *sources*. That's what spies and secret agents call them. Or sometimes *contacts*. You have *contacts* or *sources* or—hey!" Toby shouted when Ellie, taking advantage of how distracted Toby was by being a know-it-all, dove for the notepad and snatched it up. To her surprise, it wasn't a drawing of anything that could get Toby in trouble—like when he and the other neighborhood boys sometimes drew butts in class.

"Hey! What's this?" Ellie asked. There was a picture of a door, a bunch of stuff around it, and that was it. She looked at Toby, whose cheeks were bright, bright red.

"It's dumb," he said.

"What is it?" she asked. It *might* be dumb, but she couldn't know until she knew what it was.

Toby sighed and scooted closer so he could see the drawing as he explained. "It's something I'd like to build. My little brothers are

always going into my bedroom, right? So I wanted to make some sort of security system to keep them out. They're twins, so one's always stealing my stuff and the other's always breaking it. Or sometimes they both break it."

"Hmm," Ellie said, studying the drawing.

Toby went on. "So I want to build something that blares a really loud alarm, maybe, when the door handle gets turned. Or maybe a bunch of teeny poison darts could zip from the wall and stick them right in the arm!"

Ellie nodded a little but thought maybe Toby watched too many movies. "I bet your mom wouldn't be too happy about little poison darts or a super loud alarm. But maybe something else would work..." She stopped and looked up at Toby. "Maybe we can work on this in between working on the doghouse."

"Really? You'll help me with it?" Toby said, looking relieved. "I didn't get very far on my own. You can tell, I bet. I just drew the door and some alarm ideas and then a bunch of butts on the next page."

"I can tell," Ellie said. "We can work on it tomorrow. We're basically done with the doghouse until I go get the flower paper from the . . . uh . . ." Ellie tripped over the words. What she *almost* said was they could work on it while they waited for The Presidents to finish up drawing the flower wallpaper. But she didn't think Toby would like knowing The Presidents were helping any more than they would like knowing *he* was helping. After all, even if Toby turned out to be okay, he was still one of the neighborhood boys.

Toby frowned. He wasn't dumb. "What's going on? Who is making the flower wallpaper?"

"Oh, just a . . . uh . . . friend of my mom's," Ellie said fast. This was two lies about the doghouse in two days, and she hadn't liked either of them. She changed the subject as fast as she could. "Anyway, I was saying that I bet we can work on it tomorrow afternoon, after I get the flower paper. Come on—let's work on the doghouse. I'll show you how to use sandpaper."

Together, they finished the little border, which Ellie made out of some cut-up pool noodles wrapped in ribbon, and the ramp. The ramp was just a piece of wood they laid down by the door, but she showed Toby how to rub the sandpaper back and forth so it was smooth—that way, Miss Penelope wouldn't get splinters.

"I have an idea for something Kit might really like," Ellie said. "Sprinklers."

"Sprinklers? On a doghouse?"

"Yep. Kit loves running through sprinklers," Ellie said, feeling proud of the idea. She'd had it last night while lying in bed and liked it so much she kicked the blankets away and wrote it down right there in the dark. (She couldn't read the handwriting so well the next morning, but that didn't matter because it was such a good idea, she remembered it anyway.) *None* of the doghouses they'd seen that morning had sprinkler systems, so it would be really extra special. The two of them walked around to

Toby's backyard, where the doghouse sat half-finished, its soda-can roof bright and shiny in the morning sun.

Ellie put her hands on her hips. "All right. We'll need to get a plastic pipe, or maybe a piece of garden hose or something like it. We probably shouldn't cut up your dad's garden hose for this. I did it once to my dad's when I was building a marble-slinger, and he wasn't so happy."

"Oh! I know where we can get something like a hose! Hang on," Toby said, and dashed into the house. A few moments later, he emerged, holding a rubber snake. He waggled it at Ellie.

"Nice try, but I'm not afraid of snakes," she said.

"No—it's a rubber hose! It's hollow, just like one. Will it work?" Toby asked. He sounded really excited that he'd thought this up, and maybe a little offended that she'd thought he was just trying to scare her.

Ellie studied the snake. "We'd have to put holes in it to let the water through. Is that okay?"

Toby shrugged. "I have, like, a million rubber snakes. Besides, a snake sprinkler sounds cool. I want to see you build it."

Ellie grinned and took the snake from Toby. With his help, Ellie poked some holes in the rubber snake using a nail, then strung it up on sticks attached to the doghouse. Then they jammed the hose into the rubber snake's mouth, and ta-da! Dog sprinkler. Snake sprinkler? Dog-snake sprinkler?

Whatever it was, Ellie thought it was excellent. "Huh," she said, tilting her head to the side. "It doesn't look very friendly to snakes."

"I don't think most dogs like snakes anyhow," Toby said. "But if it turns out Miss Penelope *does*, I think I've got a rubber lizard that would also work."

tap nail
into snake
to make
holes

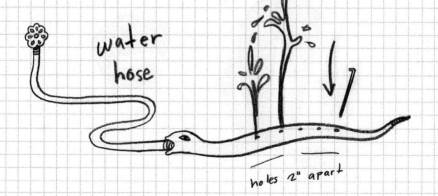

water
hose

holes 2" apart

The doghouse was looking spectacular. She and Toby high-fived, then walked around and around the doghouse, admiring their work.

"This engineering stuff is awesome," Toby admitted.

"Oh, I know," Ellie said.

Chapter Ten

The following morning, Ellie went back over to see The Presidents. She was careful not to step on the doormat—it *looked* like the Ding Dong Ditch trap wasn't set, but she didn't want to get coated in red paint powder. McKinley answered the door, with Taylor and Madison just behind her.

"Ellie! The trap worked *perfectly*!" McKinley squealed.

"Mrs. Caplan called the neighborhood boys' moms, and it turned out to be Dylan who was covered in red paint. He has to carry in all the groceries for two months!" Taylor said triumphantly.

"Wow. That's great!" Ellie said. Carrying in the groceries wasn't so bad a punishment—besides, even if Dylan *had* helped catch Muffintop, he was still Ding Dong Ditching, so it was pretty fair.

"Madison and Taylor slept over so we could finish all the roses. And so we could make cinnamon rolls. Want one?" McKinley said as they walked through the kitchen. Ellie took one from the pan and followed The Presidents down the hall.

"Okay, so, we drew a *bunch* of roses," Madison said. "But we drew some other flowers too, a little because Kit likes all kinds of flowers, but mostly because we got really tired of drawing roses."

"The doghouse is going to be the best present at Kit's party," McKinley said. "All I got her was a bunch of hair ribbons."

"Kit loves hair ribbons, don't worry," Ellie told McKinley through a mouthful of cinnamon roll.

"Yeah, but they're no doghouse," Madison said, and Ellie kept quiet, but secretly, she agreed. They turned the corner into a fancy dining room. There were markers spread across the table, and the floor was littered in construction paper. There was a neat fat stack of paper at one end, all of it shades of pink.

"So here are the drawings of the flowers," Madison said, pushing the stack toward Ellie. Ellie flipped through the drawings and her mouth fell open. The roses were *really* good. They looked a lot like the drawings in their comic books, which is to say, they looked pretty much exactly like real roses. It was way better than Ellie could have done.

"And . . . well . . ." The Presidents all looked at one another nervously. Ellie was grateful Taylor spoke up when she did.

"We have some more ideas for the doghouse," Taylor said.

"Huh?"

Taylor ran to the other side of the fancy table and grabbed a piece of paper. She held it behind her back, looking a little worried. "We don't really know a lot about engineering, so maybe not all of these ideas are good. But we just had some doghouse ideas and wanted to show you. Is that okay?"

Ellie's eyebrows raised. "Sure! Let's see."

The Presidents grinned, and Taylor put the piece of paper on the table. The four of them huddled around it.

"What do you think? Is this engineering?" Madison asked excitedly.

"Well, this is sort of just drawing," Ellie

said, thinking about how much it looked like Toby's drawing of his bedroom security system. "But it's how engineering *starts*. I always try to draw a project before I start building it."

"You think you could build this?" McKinley said excitedly.

"Um . . ." Ellie took a big breath. Some of the stuff in the drawing was pretty much impossible to build—at least, impossible to build before the party. The helicopter and its landing pad, for example, were the sorts of things Ellie figured she'd have to do a lot of research on (though, now that she thought about it, maybe if she took the motor out of the lawnmower . . .). "I don't think there's time to build *all* of this before the party, since it's only two days away—but you guys had some really good ideas, so let's think."

"Woohoo!" McKinley said, flinging her arms in the air. The other two Presidents high-fived her.

"Maybe we could build this," Ellie said, pointing to the rotating toy bin. "I think there's enough time to add the sun deck—if you guys can help me."

Madison nodded eagerly. "Of course we'll help!"

Ellie grinned—she'd wanted the doghouse to be bigger and fancier, after all! Together, she and The Presidents scouted through McKinley's house, looking for supplies. They found a laundry basket in the basement, some cardboard boxes, and an old cutting board in the yard sale pile (Ellie promised to pay fifty cents for it if McKinley's mom was mad that they took it).

"So, we'll use the cutting board as the bottom of the sun deck. But we need some Popsicle sticks, I think, for the railing," Ellie said, frowning.

"We have Popsicles!" McKinley said, and dashed to the freezer. She shook a full box of banana Popsicles at everyone. "I guess we could eat them to get to the sticks?"

It was a lot of Popsicles, but between the four of them and a whole bunch of brain freezes, they managed to eat the whole box—twenty, all together. They gathered the sticks, then went outside with all the building supplies.

"For the spinning toy bin, we'll do this," Ellie said, drawing a quick sketch. "I'll drill a hole in the bottom of the basket, then we can put it on a little post on the floor of the dog-house so it rotates," Ellie explained.

"But we don't have a post!" Madison said.

"Sure we do—we can use . . . a pencil," Ellie suggested. "Or a pen. It doesn't matter." The Presidents watched as Ellie used her drill to carefully put a hole in the center of the laundry basket. She put it on the pencil, then spun it so they could see how it would work once it was in the doghouse. "And then we'll need to cut some pieces from the cardboard so the toys stay in their little sections."

The Presidents nodded as Ellie glanced

at the clock on the microwave. Whoa! She'd been there for almost two hours—eating all those Popsicles must have taken longer than she thought.

"Can I take your drawing with me? I've got to go work on another part of the doghouse, but I want to remember what you're making over here," Ellie said.

"Sure," McKinley said, nodding. "We'll get to work cutting the cardboard out."

"I get to use the scissors!" Taylor shouted, startling everyone. But Ellie was already racing out the door.

Chapter Eleven

Ellie jogged all the way to Toby's house, holding on to the tools in her belt so they wouldn't jangle loose. When she arrived, he was drinking the day's orange soda on the back porch, fanning himself with a comic book.

"I've got the flower paper!" she called, waving it above her head as she approached him. She remembered at the last second that she was also holding The Presidents' doghouse drawing, and hurried to hide it in the back of her notebook where Toby wouldn't see it.

"Hey! These flowers look great! Your mom's friends are good artists," Toby said.

"Huh—oh!" Ellie said, remembering the lie she'd told Toby. "Right. Yep, they sure are. Let's get them put up."

"Then the doghouse is done, right?" Toby asked.

"Yep," Ellie said, and secretly thought *except the stuff The Presidents are working on,* and then felt bad about the whole thing all over again. She was almost positive Toby would love to see the toy basket, after all.

Ellie was a bit smaller than Toby, so she climbed inside the doghouse to put the flower paper up. Toby stayed at the door of the doghouse, smearing glue sticks all over the back of the paper and handing it to Ellie to paste on the walls. She lined the edges up, so it looked like real wallpaper in a real house. When they were done, she studied the house, thinking about where the rotating toy bin and sun deck would go. She wanted to tell Toby about them—they were pretty cool features, after all—and also wanted to tell The Presidents about how helpful Toby had been, especially with the snake sprinkler. But she kept her lips sealed.

"Time for my bedroom security system?" Toby asked, once all the paper was glued inside and the doghouse was drying in the sun.

"Sure," Ellie said, happy to have something else to think about. She pulled out the pencil from her own notebook and started drawing. "If you have a regular door—do you? Good. So, since you have a regular door, I was thinking we could do something like this."

"Yeah!" Toby said. "That's a great idea! What can go in the bucket? Slime?"

"I bet you'd get really grounded if you

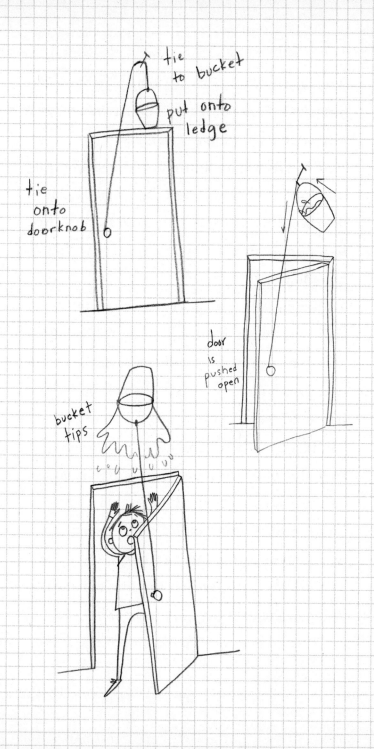

dumped slime all over the floor," Ellie said, tapping her pencil against her lips as she thought. What could they put in the bucket?

Toby frowned. "But it can't be something like . . . socks or jingle bells or tissues. It has to be something that makes them sorry they tried to snoop in my room when they know they're not allowed."

"Hmm," Ellie said. "Let's think on it. For right now, we don't need much. Just a bucket and some string. I brought some nails we can use." She pulled a handful of small nails from her tool belt pocket to prove it.

"I know where we can get a bucket and string!" Toby said eagerly. Ellie followed him to the garage, where there was a big paint bucket full of tennis balls. It didn't seem like a good idea to dump them all out in the garage, so they carried them up to Toby's room and dumped them on the other side of his bed.

Ellie had never seen Toby's room before. There were dinosaurs on the wallpaper, which Ellie thought were okay, and robots on his sheets, which Ellie thought were great—robots were the best—and she told Toby so.

"Do you think you could *build* a robot?" Toby asked, eyes wide with excitement.

"Maybe one day. But I think we'd better finish the security system before we start building robots," Ellie said.

"Oh, right. Now what?" Toby said, holding out the now-empty bucket and the rope.

Ellie carefully drilled a hole right in the middle of the bucket, then threaded the string Toby had found—it was yarn from his mom's craft kit—through. Toby, as it turned out, knew lots of knots from a report he'd done on sailors once, which he basically recited word-for-word as he tied a fancy-pants knot to hold the rope in place.

"Okay, so let's roll the chair over here," Ellie said, grabbing Toby's desk chair and pushing it over by the door. Toby held the chair steady while Ellie climbed up and nailed a single nail right in the ceiling, just above the door. He handed her the bucket, and she balanced it on the doorframe, then wound the yarn around the nail once. Toby took the other end of the yarn and tied it to the inside doorknob.

"Now we fill it with something?" Toby asked, looking excited. He rubbed his hands together.

"Not yet—we need to test it," Ellie said. "You go outside and come in. We'll see if the bucket tips over and dumps air all over your head."

"Isn't there already air all over my head?" Toby wondered as he went out. He counted down—"One! Two! Coming in!"—then pushed open the door.

The bucket, balanced on the door, tilted . . .

but then the yarn unwound from the nail and the whole thing fell. The bucket smacked down on Toby's head like a very bad hat.

"Oh," Ellie said.

"*Ow*," Toby answered, lifting the bucket up over his head. "I'll get grounded for life if I drop a heavy bucket on my brothers' heads."

"I think we need to use a *hook* instead of a nail. But I didn't bring any hooks . . . oh! Wait!" Ellie said, grabbing the pliers from her tool belt. She climbed back up on the chair, which Toby steadied as he rubbed the spot where the bucket hit him. She grabbed hold of the nail with her pliers and slowly, carefully bent it back until it was shaped like a hook.

"Whew. Okay, so now we just thread the yarn through . . . perfect! Go outside and try it again!" Ellie said.

"How about Pickles tries it instead," Toby said, grabbing hold of a big stuffed cat whose eyes had been loved off. He went outside and counted—"One! Two! Coming in! Or Pickles is, I mean!"—then threw Pickles toward the door. The weight of the stuffed cat pushed the door open, the bucket tipped, and—

"Yes! It works!" Toby said, whooping. "*Now* do we get to fill it with stuff?"

"Yep—but I have to go home for dinner. Tomorrow, can we put the doghouse on your wagon and wheel it over before lunch? We can eat at my house."

"Sure," Toby said, "lunch tomorrow." But he wasn't looking at her—he was busy rooting through his desk drawer. "Fishing worms? The plastic ones, I mean. That'd be pretty gross, but only for a minute . . . WAIT! Paper clips! No, no, that's dumb . . ."

Chapter Twelve

It was one day before the party, and Ellie felt ready. The doghouse was done—she just needed to attach the toy bin The Presidents were working on. She was meeting Toby just before lunchtime to put the doghouse in his wagon, then wheel it over to her garage. Then, she'd go over to the Caplans' house to pick up the toy bin. Kit was supposed to be off getting a party dress today, and Ellie had *really* wanted to go with her since it would mean lots of trying on dresses and jumping around the dressing room, but she wasn't quite sure she had time to spend the whole afternoon at the fancy dress shop. It was always wise, she knew, to leave some extra time when you were working on a build, just in case it all went to bees.

(Or just in case your grandma is mad and wants you to disconnect the waffle maker from the jack-in-the-box but it takes so long you have to miss ballet.)

(Even though wind-up waffles sounded like a great game *and* a great way to make breakfast or a pre-ballet snack.)

Ellie waited till she saw Kit's mom's car pull out of the driveway before hurrying out the door and down to Toby's.

"Did you figure out what to put in your security system bucket? I was thinking, maybe

Ping-Pong balls?" Ellie asked as she got closer. Toby made a few cutting motions across his throat, and soon Ellie saw why—his mom was behind him, picking peppers in her little garden.

"I have something *great* in it, but I'll tell you later," Toby whispered, giggling a little. Ellie grinned—Toby looked really happy, so it must be something great.

Together they loaded the doghouse into his wagon. It was a bit lopsided, and Ellie had to adjust one of the wheels that made it go a little sideways, but it worked just fine in the end. Once they got to Ellie's garage, they carefully unloaded it, trying their best to avoid the shingles—they were cut-up cans, after all, so they were a little sharp if you grabbed them wrong.

"Perfect," Ellie said as they walked out. She mashed the button and the garage door rattled shut behind them. "I guess it needs to be wrapped though, huh?"

"Maybe you could get a big giganto gift bag," Toby said, squinting at the sun. "Or just a bow for the top, like in the car commercials. That's how you're supposed to give giant gifts— you don't really wrap them."

"Or—"

"What's going on?" a voice interrupted. It was a high voice and sounded sort of like a voice you'd expect to hear coming out of a cartoon piece of cake. Ellie spun around. Kit was standing in her own driveway.

Ellie looked at Kit. Kit looked at Ellie. Ellie looked at Toby. Toby looked confused.

"Are you guys wearing the same clothes?" Toby finally asked. Ellie looked and, yep, she and Kit were both wearing their otter dresses, and they hadn't even planned it. The only difference was, of course, that Ellie was wearing her tool belt over hers. It looked like the otters were trying to leap into the pockets.

"I thought you had to go dress shopping," Ellie said. This probably wasn't the best thing to say, but she was so surprised she couldn't think of anything else.

Kit said, "We had to come back. Mom forgot my tights and said we can't try on dresses without proper undergarments." Toby snort-laughed at the word "undergarments." Kit gave him a look, then went on. "I thought you said you weren't playing with Toby, you were just chasing a dog." Kit didn't sound mad; she sounded *sad*. And that made it worse.

"Oh, um. I . . . ," Ellie said, but then trailed off. She couldn't tell Kit the truth—that would ruin the surprise!

"You could have just told me you wanted to play with him instead of me," Kit said, looking down.

"But that's not it!" Ellie said, her eyes going wide. "Look, I can't tell you why I fibbed, but I promise, it's a *really* good reason."

"How do I know you're not fibbing about that too?" Kit asked.

"She's not," Toby said, but the fact Toby knew this—that Toby was here at *all*—only seemed to hurt Kit's feelings more. "We're just building something together."

Now Kit looked *really* sad. "*He*'s helping you build something? Why didn't you invite me?"

"You can't help me build this thing, is all," Ellie tried to explain.

This didn't help either. Kit took a step back, then held her chin up as high as she could. Ellie could see she was trying her hardest not to sniffle. Ellie bit her lip. Maybe she should just tell Kit about the doghouse and ruin the surprise. She opened her mouth—

Kit spoke first. "I think I'll go get my dress

now. Have fun building without me," Kit said sharply, and spun around on her heel. It was her official business voice, the same one she used onstage at her pageants. It was a voice that was hard to argue with.

"Man. She was mad," Toby said as Kit disappeared.

"I should have told her about the dog-house," Ellie said. "Now she'll be mad at me until her party!"

"But then she'll be super happy when you give her the doghouse. And you'll go back to being friends, easy-peasy," Toby said.

"Maybe," Ellie said miserably, because she knew it wasn't always so easy-peasy. An apology didn't always make hurt feelings go away. She and Toby went inside her house, where she slunk through the kitchen, gathering the ingredients to make her favorite peanut-butter-marshmallow sandwiches.

"Are you sure this is a real sandwich?" Toby asked as she slathered peanut butter on some bread.

"Of course it's a real sandwich. Bread, stuff in the middle. Sandwich," Ellie said.

Toby looked unconvinced but pressed the sides of his sandwich together and took a bite. His eyes lit up. "Wow. That's a good sandwich."

"You should try it with potato chips," Ellie said.

Toby looked almost as impressed with this suggestion as he had been with the water balloon launcher. When she didn't say much else, he put his sandwich down and looked at her. "Do you think we can hook the hose up to the doghouse today, so Dylan and the McClellan twins can come see it work?"

Ellie shrugged at him. "I guess. But I'm sure we'll turn it on at the party."

"Well, yeah, but we weren't invited. It's a girls-only party," Toby said.

"What?" Ellie said, startled. It was one thing for the neighborhood boys not to be invited because they were sometimes jerk boys, but to not be invited because they were *boys*? "How can a party be girls-only? Everyone likes parties!"

Toby shrugged. "We didn't get invitations from Kit's mom—all the girls from class did, but none of the boys. Dylan says that's because it's a fancy ladies' tea party. But I really like tea! At least, I like it when you put a lot of sugar in it. Did you know they take breaks in England to have tea? Like, when they want to relax for a minute."

"You should be able to come to the party."

"It's okay," Toby said. "I mean, we didn't invite you and Kit to play soccer, because it was a boys-only team."

"That was dumb too," Ellie said. "You even said it earlier!"

"Yeah," Toby agreed. He took another big

bite of sandwich just as the doorbell rang. Ellie thought it might be Kit and ran to the door, almost crashing right into it. She flung it open.

It was The Presidents.

"Hey, Ellie! We're having some trouble with the toy bin," McKinley said. "We thought you could help."

McKinley was holding the bin—the pen the bin rotated on was crooked, and it didn't look like it would turn correctly. It was a quick fix, an easy fix, but . . .

"Um, I . . ." Ellie glanced back toward the kitchen, where Toby was waiting.

"Is the rest of the doghouse done? Can we see it?" Madison asked. Madison had a big, loud voice. Normally, it was great, especially if you were her partner on a school project where you had to talk to the class. But right now, her having a big, loud voice was a problem, because—

"Is that Kit? Is the surprise ruined?" Toby asked, and Ellie cringed as she heard his flip-flops slapping the floor as he ran her way. He rounded the corner in the hall, and his mouth dropped.

"What's *he* doing here?" McKinley asked, scowling.

"What are *they* doing here?" Toby asked, scowling back. This made McKinley scowl harder.

Ellie bit her lips, then answered everyone's question at once. "Helping with the doghouse."

And then, they all *exploded.*

Chapter Thirteen

"You didn't tell me that!" Toby shouted at the same time The Presidents yelled—almost all together—"You didn't tell us that!"

Ellie flinched. "Okay, I'm very, very sorry—it's just that I know you all don't always get along!"

"That's because he's one of the jerk boys," McKinley said.

"That's because they're gross girls," Toby answered.

"Stop it!" Ellie said. "No more name calling!" They all looked really mad, but at least they went quiet for a second.

"I can't believe you didn't tell me they were helping, Ellie. I thought we were building the doghouse together!" Toby said eventually, and now he didn't sound mad—he sounded hurt, just like Kit had earlier.

"And you lied to us," Madison said. "You told us you were building the house alone."

"You didn't even tell them I was helping?" Toby said, eyes wide.

"I just . . . I . . ." Ellie didn't know what to say or how to say it. She fiddled with one of the latches on her tool belt nervously. She could fix all sorts of things—mailboxes and fences and ladders—but she didn't know how to fix this.

"Well, *we* are leaving," McKinley said.

Madison put the toy bin on the ground. Taylor didn't let go of the scissors.

"Me too," Toby said.

"Wait!" Ellie called, but they were all on their way down the sidewalk. They split at the bottom. Toby stomped toward his house, and The Presidents stomped back toward McKinley's. None of them looked back.

Ellie sank down on the bottom step of the staircase. Her eyes felt hot and her mouth went all tight. It was one thing for one friend to be mad at her, but for *all* her friends to be mad at her? Her stomach flipped around. Why had she told so many lies to begin with? Even if they hadn't wanted to help with the doghouse, at least they wouldn't all be stomping off.

Ellie sniffed and wiped her nose on the hem of her otter dress. She couldn't just sit here and let everyone be mad. She had to do something—and do something fast, before being mad got settled into everyone's bones.

She stood up, tightened the loop holding her hammer in her tool belt, and jogged after Toby. By this point, he had a pretty big head start, and apparently he was a fast stomper. She turned onto his street just in time to see him opening his front door.

"Toby! Wait!" she yelled, but he didn't hear her (or maybe, she worried, he was so mad he was pretending not to hear her). Ellie sped up and crashed through Toby's front door without even knocking. "Toby?" she shouted in the foyer.

"Huh? Ellie?" Toby answered. He sounded confused, and he also sounded like he was in his bedroom. Ellie went up the stairs two at a time, which Kit's mom always said was unladylike, but an emergency was no time to be ladylike anyway. "Stop, Ellie!" Toby called.

"No, wait! We have to talk!" Ellie shouted back. She grabbed hold of the doorknob.

"Stop!" Toby yelled again. But it was too late. Ellie pushed open Toby's bedroom door.

At this point, Ellie remembered two things: Toby had a room security system, and Toby had never told her what great thing he'd found to put in the bucket for his security system.

She felt the door catch the string and looked up just in time to admire how well the bent nail was holding—before the bucket tipped forward and its contents rained down on her head.

"Look out!" Toby yelled from behind her.

"*Ahhhhhhh!*" Ellie screamed. Because the thing Toby had filled the bucket with was . . .

Bugs.

Roly-polies, mostly, but also fat, fuzzy caterpillars and some black beetles and at least one of the big grasshoppers with giant mirror eyes. They *chirr*ed and *skritch*ed as they hit her and the ground and began to hurry away, like they all had very important bug meetings to get to.

Ellie wasn't typically afraid of bugs—in fact, they were pretty incredible engineers, especially ants—but a surprise bug shower was enough to make just about anyone freak out. She scrambled and dusted off her dress and her hair and her dress again, and *how were there so many bugs?*

"I can help! Wait!" Toby shouted, and ran over to her. He had a broom in one hand and began to knock it against her legs. Ellie shook her head fast, and roly-polies confettied to the ground.

"What's going on up here?" Toby's mom shouted, coming up the stairs. "Is something wrong—*ahhhhh!*"

Toby's mom was quick for a grown-up. She looked from Toby to Ellie, then grabbed hold of both of their arms in a crazy-tight mom-grip.

"We've got to get out of here!" she yelled,

pulling them toward the steps. "It's an infestation! Toby, get your brothers—we have to call an exterminator!"

"Wait, Mom!" Toby said, trying to pry her hand free. "It's not an infestation!"

"There were hundreds! *Thousands*, maybe!" his mom said, shaking her head. "Where's my phone?"

"It was a security system!" Ellie said. "You don't have an infestation. Or, at least, you didn't. I guess you might now."

Finally, Toby's mom stopped. She turned around and faced the two of them. "What?"

Toby sighed. "Ellie helped me build a security system to keep Devon and Connor out of my room. It was a bucket—"

"That he was *supposed* to fill with something like Ping-Pong balls—" Ellie interrupted.

"But I decided Ping-Pong balls wouldn't freak the twins out enough, so I filled it with bugs. They mostly stayed in the bucket, and I only got the safe kind! I swear, there's not a single spider in there. Though maybe that's a way we could get rid of the bugs? Some types of spiders can eat over a dozen bugs in a single day—"

"*You filled my house with bugs on purpose?*" Toby's mom shrieked.

Ellie was pretty surprised Toby's mom didn't ground him for the rest of his life. Instead, she said she needed to take a long bath, and when she got out she'd better not see so much as a single bug leg in her house. Ellie figured she needed to stay and help, since the security system part was her fault, even if the bug part totally was *not*.

"I guess I didn't think it through, huh?" Toby said, trying to grab some of the caterpillars from the ground with his hands. "This will take forever."

Ellie frowned, looking around his room. "Maybe I can build something . . ."

"A bug trap? Will it hurt them?" Toby asked, looking concerned.

"Of course not," Ellie said. She grabbed two comic books from Toby's desk and stared at them for a moment. *These'll work, I bet*, she thought, pulling out her notebook. She drew:

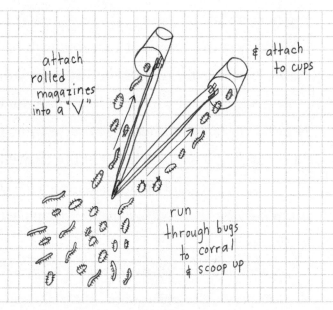

attach rolled magazines into a "V"

& attach to cups

run through bugs to corral & scoop up

"Hey! That's great!" Toby said. Then, a little quieter, "Sorry I dumped bugs on your head."

"Sorry I lied to you about The Presidents. And to The Presidents about you."

"It's okay," Toby said.

"It's okay about the bugs too. Or, at least, it will be. Once we build this. And once I take a shower."

Together they rolled up two magazines into tight tubes, put two ends together so it made a V, and taped it all up so it'd stay that way. Then Ellie emptied two pencil cups from Toby's desk, and stuck them to the wide ends of the V. She ran it across the floor, and just like she'd hoped, the bugs tumbled down the side of the V and into the cups. Toby, meanwhile, caught the flying and jumping bugs with a net. After an hour, which was still before Toby's mom got out of her bath, they'd dumped all the bugs (or, at least, all the ones they could find) outside.

"Well," Ellie said.

"Well," Toby answered. He shuffled his feet and looked sad.

"I guess I'll . . . see you?" Ellie said.

"Yeah. Around. I guess," Toby answered. "Have fun at the party tomorrow. Drink lots of tea for me."

"Okay," Ellie said, and she meant it, even though she didn't really like tea that much.

"And thanks for teaching me about engineering," Toby added.

"Anytime," Ellie said, but as soon as she said it, she realized she was lying again, without even meaning to. After all—was she really going to be able to build with Toby "anytime"? What if it made Kit mad? What if it meant she couldn't build with The Presidents? She sighed, waved at Toby, and started home.

One fewer person mad at her, but somehow, Ellie didn't feel any better.

Chapter Fourteen

When Ellie got home, she got ready for bed super early—getting ready for bed always made her feel better, even if she wasn't tired enough to actually go to bed. After taking a shower (with lots of extra shimmery body wash, on account of the bugs), she put on her favorite pajamas, the ones with the toast and purple stars on them, even though they were really more wintertime pajamas. Then she went to her bedroom window. Kit's window, which was right across from Ellie's, was open, but the curtains were closed. Ellie picked up the flashlight she kept by her bed and *flash-flash-flash*ed it at Kit's window. This was their code—three flashes was "Come to the window." Two flashes was "Come over." One flash was "Hey" or "Bye" or "Haha you're trying to sleep but I'm flashing this light at your window."

Nothing happened.

Ellie flashed another three times, then three again. Finally, Kit appeared at the window. Her hair was all fluffy and her eyes were still sad.

Ellie waved, then ducked down and grabbed her walkie-talkie, holding it up so Kit would know to turn hers on. Kit sighed (Ellie could tell by the way her shoulders went saggy) but picked up her walkie and turned it on.

"Come in, Kit. Over," Ellie said into her walkie. You had to say "over" when you finished talking on a walkie-talkie, though Ellie wasn't exactly sure why.

"Kit here. Over," Kit answered. She sounded as unhappy as she looked.

Ellie took a big breath. "Kit, I promise, promise, *promise* I wasn't leaving you out on purpose. And you'll see what I mean soon. You *have* to believe me, Kit. I'm your best friend!"

There was a long silence. Kit blinked at Ellie from across the yards.

"Oh—right. Over," Ellie finished.

"I believe you," Kit said. "But you could have told me that to start with. You still lied to me. Over."

"I know. I'm sorry. Over."

Kit didn't say anything.

Ellie didn't say anything either.

"I guess," Kit said slowly. "I just worried

that maybe you wanted to play with Toby now because he's a boy, and sometimes you like Boy Stuff. And I usually like Girl Stuff, like tea parties. Maybe you don't want to be my friend anymore. Over."

Ellie's eyes went big. That was ridiculous! Besides, like her dad was always saying, *"There's no such thing as Girl Stuff or Boy Stuff. There's only Ellie Stuff and Not-Ellie Stuff."* Building was Ellie Stuff. Tea parties were Ellie Stuff. Kit was Ellie Stuff. But Toby, now that she'd spent the day with him, might be Ellie Stuff too.

"I would never stop being your friend," Ellie said. "For one, all of our clothes match, so it'd be weird if we matched all the time but *weren't* friends. But also, just because I do something with Toby doesn't mean I *don't* want to do things with you. And *also* also, I like building, so it isn't Boy Stuff. And Toby likes tea parties, so they aren't Girl Stuff."

"Toby likes tea parties?" Kit said skeptically. She fiddled with the cord on her curtains.

"Yep. He's sort of sad he wasn't invited to yours tomorrow. Your mom only invited the girls," Ellie said.

"Oh. Well. Maybe . . . maybe Toby can come. I guess you're allowed to bring a guest to a party," Kit said. "Well—*if* he makes up for not letting us play soccer. Because that was pretty jerk boy of him."

"True," Ellie said. "Okay. I'll tell him. See you tomorrow?"

"Yep. Oh wait—over. We've been forgetting to say 'over.' Over," Kit said.

"You're right. Okay. Tomorrow. Over."

"Bye. Over."

"Bye. Over."

Ellie put the walkie-talkie away, then lay in bed for a moment, thinking. What could Toby do to make up for being a jerk boy? He could apologize, of course, and Ellie knew he would—he'd apologized to her, after all—but Ellie knew Kit needed something bigger than an apology. In fact, Ellie had a feeling Kit still needed something bigger than an apology from *her*. Was a doghouse with a snake sprinkler big enough? Ellie wasn't sure.

She reached for her nightstand, where her tool belt was sitting, and pulled out her notepad and the flat pencil. She waggled the pencil over the page, waiting for an idea, a way to fix everything, to come to her.

Nothing.

Nothing.

Nothing.

Unless . . .

Ellie had an idea—an idea that was either *really* good (like putting a big, flat piece of wood in her favorite climbing tree to lie down on) or *really* bad (like trying to build a real merry-go-round and taking apart the lawnmower to use the engine, but then not being able to put it back together . . . and also the merry-go-round caught fire and the fire department had to come and she got super grounded). Ellie got out of bed and hurried down the hall to where her mom was reading a book in the good chair.

"Mom, I need to use some of my phone calls."

"Huh?" her mom asked, looking up at her.

"I've cleaned my room and not slammed any doors for weeks now, and I even ate that white chicken chili sauce every day last week," Ellie said. "I need to call Taylor, Madison, and McKinley. Except really, only McKinley, since they're probably all having a sleepover at her house."

"It's after dinner," her mom said, shaking her head. "Maybe tomorrow morning."

"It's an emergency! It's for the project I'm building for Kit's birthday," Ellie explained.

"Please? I never use my phone calls! I have at least seven and I only want to use *one*!"

"All right, all right," her mom said, and handed Ellie her cell phone. Ellie hurriedly called McKinley. Mrs. Caplan answered, but when Ellie explained it was about Kit's party, she put McKinley on the phone.

"Hey," Ellie said. "Don't hang up! I know you're all there, and I know you're all mad at me. But look—I need your help with the dog-house. *Kit* needs your help. Tomorrow, come two hours early to the party, but come to my house instead of Kit's, okay?"

"Huh? Why?" McKinley said. She didn't sound convinced.

"Because, we have to finish the toy bin! I know you're mad at me, but this is for *Kit*. Okay?"

McKinley grumbled, and Ellie heard Madison *tsk*-ing in the background. "Fine, we'll be there," McKinley said.

"Perfect!" Ellie said. She hung up the phone and grinned. This was worth all those foods with sauces. Ellie dashed upstairs and began to leaf through her notepad.

This was going to be a *really* big build.

Chapter Fifteen

Ellie woke up early and went to Toby's house. She knocked hard on the front door. Toby's mom came to the door, looking sort of bleary.

"Can I help you?" she asked. "Oh. You didn't bring more bugs, did you?"

"Nope, bug-free! Is Toby here?" Ellie said.

"He's asleep, I think," Toby's mom said.

"I'm awake," Toby said, surprising them both. He was at the top of the stairs, wearing pajamas with fish on them. He still had pillow lines on his face. "Ellie? Is something wrong with the doghouse?"

"Nope—but meet me at my house in fifteen minutes—and bring the other neighborhood boys. We have work to do!" Ellie said triumphantly. Toby's mom blinked at Ellie, like she wasn't totally sure Ellie existed. But Toby spun around and ran upstairs. Ellie, meanwhile, returned home and raised the garage door. The doghouse was inside. She opened her notepad and tore out all the bits of the doghouse design, then untucked The Presidents' drawing from where she'd hidden it away in the back.

"Ellie! We're here. What's going on?" Toby called as he and the neighborhood boys jogged up the drive.

"Whoa," Dylan said when he suddenly saw all the pages. Ellie had laid them out on the ground, one right after another (all while trying not to look too closely at Dylan's hair, which was still a little bit red from the paint trap).

"That's a lot of doghouse," one of the McClellan twins said.

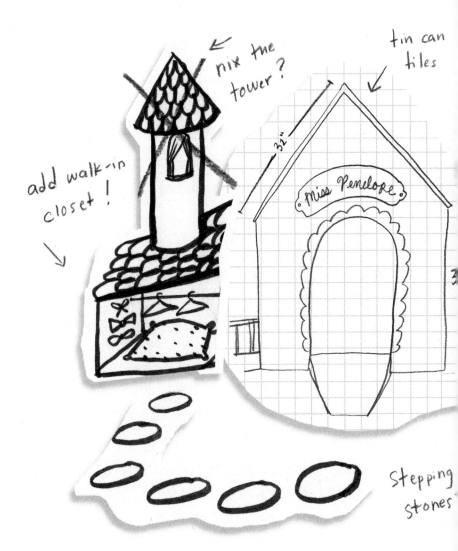

"We get to help build it now?" the other McClellan twin said.

Ellie nodded. "*Everyone* will need to help if we're going to pull this off. A few more people

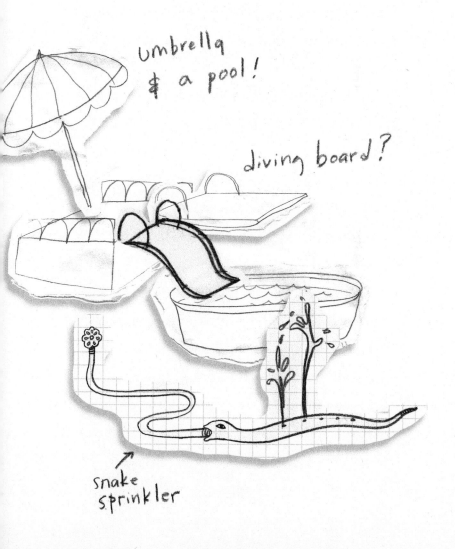

umbrella
& a pool!

diving board?

snake
sprinkler

should be arriving—there!" Ellie pointed. A van had just pulled into Ellie's driveway. Madison, McKinley, and Taylor hopped out. They were already dressed for the party, which meant they were wearing their fanciest dresses and lots of pretend jewelry. Madison even had some pretend gold and silver tattoos on her hands.

"What are these *girls* doing here?" Dylan said. "Wait! McKinley Caplan got me in big trouble!"

"You got *yourself* in trouble for Ding Dong Ditching. And what are all these jerk boys doing here?" McKinley asked, crossing her arms.

"*Everyone* is here to help build the doghouse for Kit!" Ellie said. "Look, I'm sorry I lied to you, Madison and Taylor and McKinley. And Toby, you already know I'm sorry. And McClellans and Dylan, you don't even know what I'm talking about, but it doesn't matter.

Because we can either all be mad that boys are here or that girls are here, or we can get to work and finish what we started together. Kit deserves a really amazing doghouse, and we can make it before the party if we get to work *now*."

"We're not even invited to the party," Toby said, looking sad.

"I'm inviting you," Ellie said. "I'm allowed. I'm invited, and that's how it works. You can bring a guest to parties. So Toby, you're my guest. And Dylan, you're Madison's guest. See?"

"I'm not sure that's really how it works," McKinley said.

Ellie ignored her and pointed at the sketches. "Here's what we need to do."

She divided up the work between them: Dylan and McKinley handled the pool—since they wouldn't be able to get into Kit's backyard and dig a hole for the pool, they had to improvise with a big wash bucket that Ellie built a deck around. Toby followed Ellie's directions and built a sun deck, while Madison and Taylor worked on a waterslide. One of the McClellan twins painted the molding (he was a little sloppy about it, but it looked nice all the same) while the other attached the walk-in closet and strung rope lights through it. Everyone was working together, which was good, because time was ticking away. By the time Ellie's dad brought them all sodas and peanut butter crackers as a snack, there were only thirty minutes left before the party. Ellie took out her drill to zip up a few remaining screws as Toby tucked an old comforter inside the doghouse.

They all stepped back.

"Is it done?" McKinley asked. There was a little bit of dirt smudged on her nose. Dylan's hair was sticking up with sweat. Everyone was a little out of breath.

Ellie looked at the doghouse. Was it finished?

Sometimes this was the hardest part of a build—knowing when it was complete. It was a pretty amazing doghouse, she had to admit. There wasn't another one like it on the block, to say the least. Ellie suspected there wasn't another one like it *anywhere*, which made it even cooler.

But still, Ellie was worried. She was worried about Kit forgiving her for the lie. She was worried Kit still wouldn't see that boys and girls could all like the same stuff or different stuff or some of both and it didn't matter; they could be friends anyhow. She was (really) worried Kit's mom would freak out when she and the other girls brought a bunch of boys to the ladies' tea party.

You can worry about it or you can do it! she thought to herself, which was something her mom always said.

"Let's get it to Kit's house!" Ellie said.

Chapter Sixteen

They loaded the doghouse onto Toby's wagon, then threw a bunch of strips of wrapping paper over it to make it look more like a present. It looked more like a wrapping paper monster, all uneven and lumpy and on a wagon, but it was still a nice touch. Before they started off, Toby ran back to his house and returned wearing a suit jacket and a top hat.

"Where did you get a top hat?" Ellie asked, impressed.

"Everyone should own a top hat," Toby said plainly. The other boys (and McKinley) were a little sad they didn't have one.

They wheeled the doghouse down Ellie's driveway, then back up Kit's—some of them had to push it from the back since it was so heavy now, but they were all cheering and chattering anyway. When they reached the door, Ellie turned around and shushed everyone, then knocked politely.

Kit's mom opened the door. She was wearing all black, with a fancy hat and a bunch of pearls. She was smiling and holding a pretty pink teacup.

Or, at least, she was smiling until she saw it was Ellie—with a wrapping paper monster and four boys—and that McKinley was wearing Toby's top hat, and they were all sort of smudgy and sweaty.

"What is this?" Kit's mom asked.

"We all built a present for Kit together!" Ellie explained. She was so proud—prouder than she'd been for any project before. Never in her life had so many people helped with a build!

"That's for *me*?" Kit asked, appearing behind her mother. Kit looked beautiful. Her hair was in a big pile of curls on top of her head, and she was wearing her Miss Auburn-Opelika crown with a giant fluffy pink dress. She had on shoes that were probably plastic but were clear and looked like glass, with little heels. She was even wearing pink nail polish.

"Ellie designed it, and we all built it," Toby said brightly.

Kit's mother made a noise in her throat.

"Thank you so much! Bring it around to the backyard!" Kit said excitedly, bouncing up and down. She raced through the house and around the yard to unlock the fence. Ellie and the others pulled hard to get the wagon through the deep part of the grass. They parked it on the patio, right in front of the giant Happy Birthday, Kit sign Kit's little sister and stepdad were hanging up. There were already tables set up with pink placemats and pink teacups and fancy trays with finger sandwiches on them.

"Wow! High tea!" Toby said, and sat down. He folded his napkin in his lap neatly, then poured himself a cup of tea. When he went to drink it, he held his pinky finger out.

"Oh. What nice manners," Kit's mom said, and sat down beside him. "Why don't we go ahead and do presents now, so we can get that . . . *erm* . . . wagon out of the way?"

"Yes! Presents, please!" Kit said excitedly, looking at Ellie. "Should I open yours first?"

"Absolutely," Ellie said.

Everyone gathered around the wagon. The

kids looked at one another eagerly, waiting to see the look on Kit's face. She peeled back layer after layer of wrapping paper, then gasped.

"It's *beautiful*!" she said.

"What is it?" her mom said.

"It's a doghouse!" Ellie exclaimed. "Let's get it set up, guys!"

Ellie, Toby, and the others hurriedly lifted the doghouse out of the wagon. They put up the umbrella and the pool and the little extra room off the main bit. "It's a dressing room—like you have at pageants! See, I even put a light in there!" Ellie explained. Toby dashed to the hose and filled up the pool, and within a few minutes, they were all standing proudly beside it, pointing out all the features so Kit wouldn't miss anything.

"We did the shingles here," one of the McClellans said.

"And we did the waterslide," Madison said, motioning to herself and Taylor.

"But it was all Ellie's design. She drew the whole thing up and gave us jobs," Toby said, and Ellie beamed. Kit bounded over and hugged Ellie tightly.

"Thank you, thank you, *thank you*," Kit said.

"You're welcome! I'm so sorry I lied, Kit," Ellie said quietly so only Kit could hear her. "And tell your mom I'm sorry I brought so many extra people to the party, because I don't think she's very happy about it."

"I'm not mad anymore. How could I be mad when you built me a doghouse with a *dressing room*?" Kit said happily. She looked over at the other party guests. "And I don't think my mom is *that* mad. Besides, I think Toby likes tea parties even more than her." She whispered this last bit and nodded her head toward Toby. He was still circling the doghouse proudly but had retrieved his teacup and took a small sip every few steps. Ellie and Kit quiet-fived (which is like a regular high five, but you just press your palms together so there's no sound and no one knows you're saying "*WOOHOO!*" in your head).

"A doghouse, eh?" Kit's mom said. "And how would Ellie have known you might need a doghouse? Were you two snooping?"

Kit and Ellie looked at one another.

"We were . . . um . . . ," Kit said.

"Lying does *not* become a lady," Kit's mom said. She sighed. "Well. I guess that means you *think* you know Kit is getting a dog."

Ellie's stomach started to slowly, slowly sink. No. It couldn't be. Miss Penelope *was* coming, right? She looked at Kit, whose eyes were wide with worry. Now that Ellie thought about it, they'd never heard Kit's mom say the word "dog." They'd never heard her say anything about a pet. They'd only heard her say the name "Miss Penelope." What if Kit's mom had just gotten Kit a fancy doll? Or a pretend dog? Or some sort of robot dog?

(*On second thought, a robot dog would be pretty awesome*, Ellie thought.)

(*No! Nothing is as cool as the real Miss Penelope!*)

"Well. You sure are going to be surprised," Kit's mom said. Kit looked stricken. Ellie looked sick. "Everyone close your eyes, so I can go get the family's present to Kit."

They all shut their eyes—McKinley pulled Toby's top hat down over hers. Before they did, Kit grabbed Ellie's hand and squeezed it tightly.

"It's okay if it's not a real dog," Kit said. "We can still have fun with the doghouse. We can pretend there's a dog, and the pool is big enough for our feet, so I'll teach you how to do fancy pedicures." She was talking fast, trying to make everything a-okay. "Besides, it'll be a good thing to have if I ever get a dog—"

"*Surprise!*" Kit's mom said. "Oh. Looks like she's being a bit shy."

Everyone's eyes sprang open. Kit's mom was standing at the door, holding a leash—and whatever was at the end of that leash was hiding behind her. Even though they couldn't see what was attached to the leash, it was clear it was something real, alive, and dog-size!

"*Ahhhhh!*" Kit squealed. It *was* Miss Penelope!

"*Ahhhhh!*" the other kids said.

"*Baaahhhh!*" said the dog behind Kit's mom's legs.

"Wait," Ellie said, confused. "Dogs *bark*." At that exact moment, Miss Penelope butted her way out right through the middle of Kit's mom's knees.

Miss Penelope was not a dog.

Miss Penelope was a lamb.

A white lamb, with a downy coat and a little V-shaped nose and beetle-black eyes. Her hooves—hooves!—clattered on the patio stones as she bounded into the middle of the party.

"Wait, is that a sheep? Or like a really weird breed of dog?" Dylan asked as Kit ran forward. She slid to her knees, ruffling up her dress. Kit wrapped her arms around Miss Penelope, squealing.

"*Baaaahhhh*," Miss Penelope said, breaking free. She hopped up and down, twisting in the air like this was a really fun game.

"That *is* a sheep!" Madison said.

"Technically, she's a miniature cheviot," Kit's mom said, looking a bit offended that anyone would call Miss Penelope a mere *sheep*. "She's been bottle fed and is hypoallergenic, so she won't make your sister or father sneeze."

"I *love* her!" Kit said. When she jumped back, Miss Penelope jumped and kicked playfully. It was pretty much the most adorable thing Ellie had ever seen.

Ellie and Toby looked at each other. What did this mean for their present?

"Come on, Miss Penelope! Come look at your house!" Kit said, and ran toward the doghouse. Miss Penelope bounded along after her and, to everyone's surprise, leaped right onto the roof. She pranced around there for a moment before hopping down and ducking inside, bleating happily.

"She likes it!" Kit said excitedly.

Ellie looked at the others. "Nice work, everyone."

"Nice design, Ellie," Toby answered, sipping his tea. "What are we building next?"

Ellie took out her notepad and wrote, *Project 62: SHEEPhouse.* Then she looked up at the others and said, "Let's think."

Project 62: <u>SHEEP</u>house

ELLIE'S VERY FAVORITE TOOLS

(A GUIDE)

Safety Glasses

Builds can get sort of crazy, sometimes—little wood chips or screws or pieces of rope or who-even-knows-what flying everywhere. Wearing safety glasses is really important so nothing pops you in the eye. Also, they make you look super official and fancy.

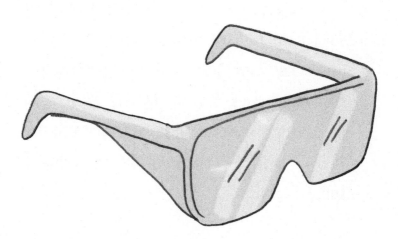

Hammer

If you want to nail something together—which is called *driving* a nail—you've got to have a hammer. You definitely want a hammer that feels right to you—so it might be one that's different from your best friend's hammer. Like, maybe yours is a little heavier, or a teeny bit smaller. You should be able to swing it nice and easy when you're driving a nail. You don't want to have to wallop the top of the nail crazy hard; just hold it between your fingers and give it a *tap-tap-tap* to drive it in. Be super careful when hammering stuff. If you miss and hit your finger it hurts super bad.

The back of the hammer—the side with the metal "V"—is what you use for removing nails if you've changed your mind about whatever you're building (which happens a lot). Just put the top bit of the nail in the "V," and then pry down, and the nail should pop right out.

Screwdriver

Screwdrivers come in all sorts of shapes and sizes, and they're for driving screws—which are sort of like nails, only they twist into stuff. The first thing you need to know is that there are two main types of screwdrivers—*Phillips head* and *flat head*. A flat-head screwdriver is flat at the top of the metal part. A Phillips-head one has a little "X" mark at the top of the metal part. You use a flat-head screwdriver to drive flat-head screws, and a Phillips-head screwdriver to drive Phillips-head screws. Makes sense, right?

A lot of things are put together with screws—some with big, giant screws, and some with screws so tiny that if you sneeze while looking at them, they'll get lost. If you want to put in a screw or remove a screw, you just need to remember this: *lefty loosey, righty tighty.* So, if you want to loosen a screw and remove it, spin the screwdriver to the left. If you want to tighten a screw, turn it to the right.

Drill

This is one of the best tools in the entire world, because it makes life *so much easier.* A drill is basically an electric screwdriver—you can drive screws way faster with it, and remove them way faster too. That's not the only thing it does, though—drills come with a lot of different *drill bits,* which is the part that fits into the screw. So, you don't need a bunch of different drills the way you might need a bunch of different screwdrivers—you just need a bunch of little drill bits.

But you can also get bits that do things other than drive screws—like put holes in things, or mix things. And you can get bits that drive screws into strong stuff like bricks or metal.

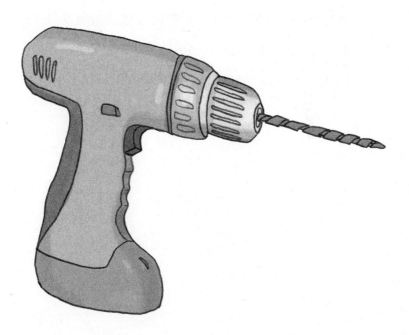

Tape Measure

You're going to need a tape measure for just about any build. A tape measure is for measuring how long or deep or wide something is—just pull out the little metal part (it's usually yellow) and line it up on whatever you're measuring. A good rule is to always measure twice—because if you measure wrong and start putting something together, you'll have to take it all apart and start over!

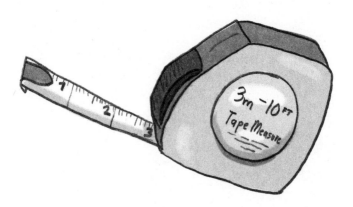

Wrench

There are probably a million different sizes and types of wrenches, sort of like screw-drivers. Wrenches are used for removing bolts—which are sort of like six-sided screws. You just put the open part of the wrench on the bolt, and turn (*lefty loosey, righty tighty!*). Lots of times wrenches and bolts are used for big stuff, like holding together a playset or a car.

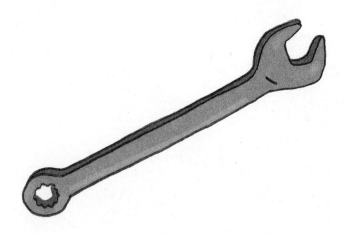

What will be Ellie's next fantastic
engineering project?

Read on for a sneak peek to find out!

Ellie Bell was building something new.

This wasn't weird or anything, because Ellie was basically *always* building something new. It was pretty much her favorite thing to do, especially during the summer: come up with a new project, design it, then build it with her friends Kit and Toby.

What *was* weird about this particular

something new was the fact that it involved twenty-four jars of bread-and-butter pickles.

"Does it still look flat to you?" Ellie called out to Toby. Toby was in Ellie's playhouse, which doubled as her workshop—it was full of tools and bits of wood and loose screws she'd collected in peanut butter jars. Right now, Toby was staring out the playhouse window, narrowing his eyes at the scuffed-up tabletop they'd found in someone's trash a few days ago. Kit didn't like it so much when Ellie got excited about something from the trash—Kit was a very tidy person—but Ellie knew sometimes people threw away really, really useful stuff.

The tabletop had two ropes—one on each end—that were knotted together in the middle. Right now, it was hovering just an inch or so off the ground, so Ellie could make sure it stayed nice and flat in the air.

"It looks flat to me," Toby called back down,

putting his hands around his mouth to make his voice louder.

"What about from there?" Ellie asked Kit, who was standing on the porch, looking at the tabletop through pink binoculars, even though she wasn't really that far away from the workshop. Kit was wearing a T-shirt that had a dog wearing heart-shaped sunglasses on it. Ellie was wearing the same one—they'd decided the T-shirts were lucky, since whenever they were wearing them, they built something really good, or the ice-cream truck came around the neighborhood, or they wrote a really funny joke together.

"We're go for flat!" Kit answered, waving a thumbs-up in the air.

"Great!" Ellie said. She climbed the ladder up to her workshop and nudged Toby over a little bit. Right by the door, there was a chain from Toby's old swing set. It went out the playhouse door and to a piece of the workshop roof, where Ellie had it looped around a back wheel from her old tricycle—one without the tire—then down to the tabletop. The tricycle wheel with the rope made a pulley! Pulleys were machines, just very simple ones—but that didn't make them any less cool, because they made it way easier to lift super-heavy things up into the air.

"Most elevators don't use swing-set chains," Toby said, shaking his head. That's what this build was—an elevator for the workshop. Once it was done, Ellie wouldn't need to make a billion trips up and down the ladder to take things into her workshop. *And* it would be a way for people who couldn't climb the ladder, like her grandma or Lacey from school (who had a glittery pink wheelchair), to get up into the workshop if they wanted to come visit.

"Well, most elevators are for much taller buildings," Ellie pointed out. "And they *do* use pulleys, like we're using. Just lots of really giant pulleys instead of one made out of a tricycle wheel."

Toby nodded, looking thoughtful. "That's true. I looked it up last night, and most elevators have to be inspected. Do you have an inspector coming? You can schedule an inspector on weekdays, according to the website I saw."

Toby got like this now and then. People in class sometimes called him a know-it-all—Ellie, in fact, used to call him that a lot. She didn't really anymore, though, because now she knew that Toby was just *Toby*, just like she was just Ellie and Kit was just Kit. It didn't seem right to be friends with Toby but still call him a name behind his back, even if he did still make her sigh a little here and there.

"Maybe *you* can be the inspector," Ellie suggested, taking hold of the chain.

"I do know a lot about elevators, now," Toby said, looking pleased. He folded his arms and pulled in his eyebrows, and Ellie had to admit, he did look very inspector-y.

"Perfect!" Ellie said, then looked out the workshop door to Kit, who was watching birds through her binoculars. "Keep an eye on it, Kit!" Ellie yelled. "Ready? One, two, *three!*"

On three, she pulled back on the chain. It slid through the tricycle-wheel-pulley and tightened all the way down to the tabletop. She pulled some more, and the tabletop began to rise off the ground, inching up toward the workshop. When it was level with the floor, Ellie stopped, then wrapped the chain around a high-heeled shoe she'd nailed to the floor (it made a handy doorstop and didn't hurt your toes when you stepped on it barefoot).

"Woohoo!" Kit cheered from below.

"Inspection part one, passed!" Toby said, and high-fived Ellie. She grinned. Building projects were always better when Toby and Kit were with her.

"Are we ready for these?" Kit asked, nudging a thick-sided cardboard box with her toe. It was stacked two rows high with glass jars of pickles that said *In a Pickle* in swirly writing on the side. They'd found the box and the pickles in Kit's garage, and Ellie had done a little math: Each jar of pickles weighed two and a half pounds. She, Kit, and Toby all weighed about sixty pounds each. So, if the elevator was strong enough to lift twenty-four jars of pickles—which was every single jar—it could definitely lift a person. Ellie thought it was pretty lucky how quickly they'd found something to test the elevator with. Sometimes engineering just worked out like that!

"Sure, let's do it!" Ellie answered Kit's

question. Really, she knew they ought to test the elevator with one jar of pickles at a time, just to be safe . . . but the first test had gone so well! Besides, the sooner they proved *all* the pickles could be lifted, the sooner they could start riding up and down on the elevator themselves.

Ellie and Toby hurried down the workshop ladder. The three of them began to haul the jars of pickles out of the box and onto the tabletop—onto the *elevator*—stacking them up neatly. Toby even made sure all the labels were facing the same way, like they do at the grocery store. When they were done, and the summer sunshine was hitting the pickles just right, it looked like the jars were filled with magical green potion.

Well, pickles in magical green potion, anyway.

Ellie checked the knots, then pulled her hammer from her tool belt and tap-tap-tapped

on the nails holding the tabletop together, just to double-check they were all good. Yep—all the knots were so tight, they were like little rocks made of rope.

It was elevator time.

The three of them scrambled back up the workshop ladder, Kit and Toby poking their heads out the windows on either side of the door so they could get a good view of the build in action. Ellie took a deep breath— the excited kind, with just a little bit of the nervous kind way in the back of her throat— and grabbed hold of the chain.

"*Oof*," she said, pulling back.

Pickles were really heavy when there were twenty-four jars of them stacked together. The elevator had barely moved an inch off the ground.

"*Oooooooof*," Ellie said, pulling back even harder.

"I thought the pulley was supposed to make it easy to lift," Kit said, frowning. "Here, let me try."

Kit was pretty strong, so Ellie handed over the chain. She pulled with her whole body, but the elevator hardly moved. Toby didn't have any luck either.

"Maybe we ought to try together?" Kit said thoughtfully, and took the chain from Toby's hands. Kit, Toby, and Ellie all grabbed hold of a different section of the chain. Ellie took a breath and gripped it so tightly that it pinched her fingers.

"One, two, *pull*!" she said, and together, they hauled back on the chain. The tabletop lifted! The elevator was working!

For a second, anyway.

Then things went . . . well, *sideways*. Literally.

The tabletop suddenly tilted just a teeny

bit, but that was all it took—because before Ellie or her friends could react, the pickle jars began to *slide* down the tabletop. Ellie yelped, Kit squealed, and Toby said, "Oh, no, no, no, no, no" so fast it sounded more like he was humming than speaking.

Twenty-four pickle jars slid off the end of the tabletop. They crashed to the ground, but Ellie didn't see it happen, because as soon as they fell, the rope became light, and she and her friends tumbled backward into a heap of elbows and knees.

"This isn't good," Ellie said, rubbing the spot where she'd smacked her head on Kit's kneecap.

"Pickle juice is sometimes called *brine.* It's very acidic. It might kill the grass," Toby answered.

"Do you think they all broke? Do you think my mom will notice?" Kit said worriedly, sticking out her hands to help Ellie and Toby up. Her fingernails still had baby chicks painted on them from when she and Ellie had played nail salon the day before. Okay, they mostly looked like yellow blobs, but they were *supposed* to be chicks. Ellie just didn't understand how the people on the videos they'd watched were so good at painting pictures on such a tiny little nail.

They winced and hobbled over to the edge of the workshop and looked down.

Twenty-four jars of pickles, all cracked open, pickles strewn across the grass. The tabletop was flipped over, the ropes were tossed around like spaghetti noodles, and the pickle juice smell was extra strong and sting-y sweet in the summer air. It didn't look like a single jar of In a Pickle pickles had survived the fall.

"Maybe we should have started with pillows instead of glass jars?" Ellie suggested a

little weakly, and pulled out her notebook, flipping to the page where she'd sketched out the elevator. "Or maybe if we ... hmm ... I wonder if there's a way to keep the stuff on the elevator from wobbling—"

"Um, Ellie? I think before we fix this build, we'd better fix ... well ... *this*," Kit said, motioning to the pile of pickles with one hand and biting the nails of the other.

"I don't think we can fix this," Toby said, shaking his head.

"Well, at least clean it up?" Kit replied.

"You can't really clean it up. The brine is soaked into the dirt now. The grass is doomed."

Ellie wanted to glare at Toby because he was totally not helping, but the truth was, she felt like a lot more than the grass was doomed— especially once Kit's mom found out. She thought about the back of her notepad, where she always wrote down projects once they were finished and working and great.

She definitely would *not* be adding Project 63: Workshop Elevator to that list today.

Jackson Pearce began writing when she got angry that the school librarian couldn't tell her of a book containing a smart girl, horses, baby animals, and magic. Her solution was to write the book herself when she was twelve. Now Jackson is the author of the Ellie, Engineer series, *The Doublecross*, and *The Inside Job*, the coauthor of the Pip Bartlett series, and the author of a series of teen-retold fairy tales, including *Sisters Red*, *Sweetly*, *Fathomless*, and *Cold Spell*, as well as several stand-alone novels. She lives in Atlanta, Georgia.

www.jackson-pearce.com

@JacksonPearce